Within Our Celebration

Short Stories

by

Kieran York

Scarlet Clover Publishers, L.L.C.

Littleton, Colorado

Edited by Martha Ryan
Cover Design by Karen D. Badger
Interior Design and Formatting by Karen D. Badger
Cover Art by Bryan Boling
Interior Photography by Kathie Solie
Back Cover Photo by Brenda Starr

Published by Scarlet Clover Publishers L.L.C.

P.O. Box 621002
Littleton, Colorado 80162

Printed and bound in the United States of America, UK, and Europe

ISBN-13: 978-0692509975
ISBN-10: 0692509976

Kieran York

Within Our Celebration

Short Stories

by

Kieran York

Books also written by Kieran York:

Touring Kelly's Poem
Loitering on the Frontier
Night Without Time
Earthen Trinkets
Timber City Masks - 1 (A Royce Madison Mystery)
Crystal Mountain Veils - 2 (A Royce Madison Mystery)
Shinney Forest Cloaks – 3 (A Royce Madison Mystery)
Careful Flowers
Appointment with a Smile
Sugar With Spice (Short Fiction)
*Blushing Aspen – 2014 Sappho's Corner Solo Poets
Series (Poetry)*
Realm of Belonging – Poetry

Trevar's Team: 1(Forthcoming New Mystery Series)

Contributor to Sappho's Poetry Series, edited by Beth Mitchum

Wet Violets, Volume 2
Roses Read, Volume 3
Delectable Daisies, Volume 4

DEDICATION:

For my friend, Kathie Solie.

Kathie and I have been friends throughout the last few years.

Friends are there during high and low points. Every life has them both. Kathie seems to know (perhaps telepathy of some sort) when my writing is lagging or something in my life is a problem – unwell family or friend, whatever. Kathie reaches out in some way – her magical photos, sending a Janis Joplin stamp, or poetry book. In some way her kindness never fails to prop me up, just when I need a lift.

So thank you, Kathie. You are one of life's special and fine women. Yours is a treasured friendship.

ACKNOWLEDGEMENTS:

As always, I acknowledge Beth Mitchum.

My thanks go to all those who have assisted in building Scarlet Clover Publishers. Beth is and always will be the one that was first to help – and I'm grateful beyond words.

Others I'd like to acknowledge: The wonderful Karen D. Badger. The magnificent Rogena Mitchell-Jones. The charming Jerry L. Wheeler. And the Amazing Team – Kathie Solie, Brenda Starr, Martha Ryan, Bryan Boling, and our friends.

I'm so fortunate and blessed to be a part of the Scarlet Clover family.

My family – they have always been there for me. My sister and brother-in-law are responsible for making my life fun and fabulous. My nephews and their wives make my life a joy, and nine great-nieces and great-nephews – they make my life entertaining and energetic.

If this is a dream – please, let's not wake me. How wonderful to be a part of my family.

How wonderful to be associated with those talented and creative Scarlet Clover people listed above – and to be a part of writing and publishing among this Glorious Publishing Time.

acknowledge and am I grateful for all other Sapphic publishers and writers out there. We're making one another better!

Kieran York

Table of Contents:

Photograph by Kathie Solie

ADIE'S LAST SUPPER

"Delbert!" boomed Burgess McMurtry's rumbling voice. "Damned glad it's you arriving rather than that *dreadful* woman."

Glancing around the terrace of the luxurious Palm Springs home, Delbert Whitney already felt the loss. This place, with its plush gardens, had always been a reflection of Adeline McMurtry's joy. Her lust for life was lavish and elegant. The garden was her favorite place. There, in that enclave of tranquility, Delbert and Adie had shared brunches of champagne, flaky pastries, fresh strawberries, and laughter. There, amongst bursts of floral colors, they had staged elaborate, extravagant lawn parties.

The same style and grace had made Adeline one of Hollywood's leading fashion designers. She'd become elevated to high priestess of classic motion picture vogue. Delbert often told her that over the decade she had created more trends than any Sapphic had a right to. This always brought a lift to her eyebrows and a smile to her lips.

And over the years she had also given her famous imprint to an exclusive women's clothing line. The bolts of fabric continued rolling, and the fortunes continued rolling in. Adie had achieved a great deal in her lifetime

Delbert tucked his pocket-watch back inside his vest pocket. He had taken a seat at the oval patio table. He sighed. Compact, his slender frame now sagged slightly. He glanced at his well-manicured nails. Then his hand brushed back his neatly trimmed, salt and pepper-colored hair. His thin mustache was slightly grayer.

Above all, Delbert reflected dignity. Even in his early days of law school, decades ago, his distinguished persona was acknowledged. Fellow students called him *professor*. He believed then, and now, in constant attention to detail. His suits, vests, shoes, socks, and bow ties, were always perfectly coordinated.

"Dreadful woman?" Delbert inquired. He cleared his throat.

"About whom are you referring?"

"Binky. My sister-in-law, Binky," Burgess barked. "Hell, the vicious woman castrated my brother the moment she drug him down the aisle. Harold didn't have a prayer. Binky knows I'm hearing impaired. The bitch used to shout. Now she whispers. Wants to get her hands on Adeline's millions. If my Thelma would have known Binky was showing up for the death watch, *she* wouldn't have missed it. You remember Thelma, don't you?"

"I certainly do," Delbert responded. He recalled with rancor the buxom, shrill-voice woman. Their daughter, Tammy, was equally buxom and shrill-voiced. Adie often called Tammy the most *heterosexual* human in the species. "Yes. It's a pity Thelma didn't attend."

"Of course Thelma is devastated. The poor, old girl is *devastated*! Not that we expected Adeline to go on forever."

"One never knows, she may," Delbert uttered defensively. He recalled how Thelma had been the first family member to ostracize Adie after discovering her sister-in-law's penchant for women. Adeline had been heartbroken at Thelma's outburst. Thelma stated that Tammy Lynn must never be left alone with her *lesbian* Aunt Adeline. Adie directed the pain of rejection away, and busied herself with her career. She designed many of her most famous costumes and gowns while suffering from her family's scorn. Delbert was one of the few friends who understood Adie's hurt. "Adie has experienced enormous success in her lifetime. Her achievements have not gone unnoticed. That certainly takes a strong spirit."

"But we all die off. The doctor is in with her now. He claims she won't last the night." Burgess swirled the ice that was stacked in his glass of Scotch. His hands were trembling slightly. His large, barrel-chest heaved with each breath. His frame filled the wicker patio chair. An ash-gray face and dark dot eyes above puffs of flesh made him appear unwell. Chalk-white hair strung across his forehead. When he spied his sister-in-law strolling toward them, his face went the color of ripe plumbs. "Oh, damn. It's Binky."

"Burgess," Binky McMurtry chanted her greeting to her brother-in-law.

He stood, flinging his hands open in a welcoming gesture. "Binky, dear. How are you?"

"One learns to cope," she replied. She kissed both her brother-in-law's cheeks. With a NurtraSweet gush, she added, "And where is

Thelma?" She reached to catch her sliding poppy-golden colored hat. Easing her stick-thin figure into a chair, she removed the hat. Then she began peeling off her matching gloves. With a dramatic flip of her brass-tinted hair, above her well-stretched facial skin, her hands fluttered through the air. "Thelma hasn't fallen off the wagon *again?*" With a quick aside, she whispered to Delbert, "Drank like a guppy before her gallbladder went out on her."

Irritated, Burgess rustled in his chair. "She's helping Tammy Lynn's oldest daughter make preparations for a graduation party. Pity Adeline won't be able to attend. Of course she'd be invited."

"I haven't seen Tammy Lynn since Harold's funeral. How is *this* marriage going for her?" Binky quizzed.

"Fine. And how is Harry Junior doing with his indictment?" Burgess retaliated.

"Since his investment brokerage went under, he's had his troubles. But he's his father's son. He'll cope. Like the rest of us. And dear, dear Delbert, how are you taking all of this? After all, you've been Adeline's friend and confidant, as well as her attorney, all these many years."

"Nearly fifty," Delbert reported. He couldn't explain that the relationship went far beyond friendship. Beyond attorney-client association - for they had been quickly drawn to one another from the beginning. Adie was a struggling designer of twenty-seven when they met. He was a twenty-five year old law school graduate. They had originally been one another's 'show' for the straight world. *Beard* they had once called the charade. He attended fashion galas with her. She attended law firm functions with him.

Delbert had become her financial engineer. He converted her income into a fortune with a life of its own. Her funds were secured, amassed under his careful speculation. In return, he was granted access to her powerfully rich and famous associates. They were Hollywood's elite. They quickly became his clients.

But Delbert admitted early on his friendship with Adie was much more. They had become family. When one of his male lovers made an exit, Adeline was there. When one of her Sapphic affairs ended, his quiet humor broke the fall. Brother and sister. More family than these people, Delbert acrimoniously thought. For Adie's and his were contributing bonds. Adeline's two brothers and their families had only *taken* from her throughout the years. And now, mused Delbert, let the bricks fall in with the wall.

"Should we call a minister?" Binky questioned.

"I think not," Delbert answered. "Adie is not so inclined.

* * *

Adie felt the thick cord of silver hair that was braided at the back of her neck. She remained still, allowing Burgess and Binky to believe she was no longer lucid. She hadn't intended to eavesdrop on them. But after all, they had come to her deathbed. What could they expect? Adie was amazed they hadn't brought their entire families to string around the bed like a human rosary. She'd been spared all but two of the 24-karat, gold-plated vultures. But what a two – Burgess and Binky!

"Burgess, do you think she knows we're here?"

How could I miss Binky's singsong voice? That operatic Hallmark card intonation was Binky's alone. Binky. Binky, who once requested Adie not bring any of her dotty old 'dyke' friends with her to Harry Junior's wedding. She'd know Binky anywhere.

"She was an eccentric old gal," Burgess thundered. "Hell of a gal." He leaned over Adie. "Harold and I always loved our older sister."

Adie felt an inner smile. They were a couple of little pricks and they made her childhood a misery. They had totally rejected her until her fortune grew. Now Burgess claimed love. Now Harold's widow claimed love. It would have made her absolutely furious if it wasn't such a stitch. Imagine them, crying like a couple of coyotes. They were strangers. Strangers in life who moved past her from time to time. They were related, but they were unknown statuaries of her existence.

"Yes. My Harold and I often prayed for her. Her salvation."

Prayed! So Adie often heard. Harold and Binky made an effort to sanitize her soul. They wanted her redemption - it was in her best interest. They wanted her reformation. Rehabilitation. That was their task. They had even sent a blind date to restore her to heterosexuality. The 'date' was hardly up to the task of discouraging lesbianism.

"My Harold was so compassionate toward her indiscretions. But he was like that with everyone."

Compassionate! As a boy Harold's compassionate little foot had airlifted a neighbor's Pomeranian across the playground. When Adie chased her younger brother, she was angry enough to have broken him into bits. The chicken-shit ran like a mouse on a skateboard.

Compassionate! Both brothers should have been place in restraints for the first twenty years of their lives.

"Audio difficulties," Burgess bellowed. He fiddled with his squealing hearing aid. "Well, Adie certainly lived life to the fullest. Told me she never expected to make it past fifty."

Yes, Adie reflected, *wide open living.* She had used life to its best advantage. Not a single regret.

"I wouldn't wonder," accused Binky. "With her bad heart from that childhood rheumatic heart, her life couldn't have been easy. *And* I counted nine women lovers." Binky's eyes cast downward, closing saintly as she shook her head. "What a pity she didn't settle down with a man. She was an attractive woman. She certainly could have found someone to marry her."

"At least she had the grace and decorum to keep it undercover. Only her 'own kind' knew about the degeneracy," Burgess hooted.

I take that back. That undercover business was my one regret, Adie considered. She should have shouted it from the rooftops. She should have inked up the scandal sheets with news of her degeneracy. *Degeneracy!* Adie scowled. Had Burgess worn suspenders, he'd never have survived the whiplash as he dropped his drawers for every floozy who would have him. If it moved, he'd have it. Nine wouldn't have gotten him through a sales convention.

"Well, I'm glad they don't put those kinds of things in obituaries. List her lovers."

Oh, Binky, please! Adie released an intentional and disturbing sigh. *Why can't they discontinue the I.V. and just allow me to suffer to death quickly. Be done with it. It's almost over, why not quit this foolishness?*

"How we'll miss her," lamented Burgess.

What a load of crap! Adie's reminiscence became introspective. The years, the friends, the women, the memories all twirled in her mind. What great fortune life had provided for her! There were nine lovely, splendid women. With each of them she had exchanged diamonds. She'd told them that their love was the most majestically sparkling part of her life. And so it was.

Adie was never one to be boxed inside memories. But now, each remembrance was a fine friend. A comfort. She'd accomplished so much more than she'd originally intended. She'd acquired so many more friends than she'd believed possible. And her lovers were truly gems within her heart. How magical. How wondrous this waning life had been. And why the hell didn't Burgess and Binky leave her alone.

Scram! To retaliate for their inconsideration, she planned on asking Delbert to add an additional word on her headstone: SAPPHIC.

* * *

"Come along now, my dear old friend." Delbert watched as Adie's eyes, with pensive caution, pried open. When her smile sprouted, he laughed. "There. That's better."

"You knew!" she muttered as she rallied.

"Of course, I knew you're still rational. You sly, old kit fox. It's purely *Adeline!*"

His chuckle chained with hers. "I knew you couldn't be bothered by those two. And wouldn't be."

"I don't want them placing my corpse on a last-minute sarcophagus of guilt," she clamored. A rattling cough trailed her giggle. "And I need to save my strength for our final widdie-widdie, darling counselor."

Delbert clasped her hand. Her fingers weakly clutched back. Delbert sat in the chair next to her bed. "Yes, Adie, I'm here. Here with you."

"As you always have been. Del, darling, have you tidied things?"

"Exactly as you requested. Your funds have been liquidated. Your fortune has been distributed among the charities you listed. Remaining funds for medical and funeral expenses will be appropriated as so stipulated. And it *is* ironclad. I've seen to that." He paused, reaching into his coat's breast pocket. "And here is the jewelry you've asked me to retrieve from your safety deposit box. I've taken the nine diamonds from each of their settings." He placed the small packet of gems on the bed stand.

"And the coffin is to be sealed. No showing."

"And no autopsy. As you petitioned. All of your dictates will be carried out exactly as you've requested."

"Darling boy, you are truly the best friend I've ever had. What glorious days we've shared. My exuberance has carried me to so many lovely places. I even face the unknown with somewhat of an anticipation. Mind you," she conceded, "I would normally have allowed my competition to break their teeth on the untried. But they've all gone on to search out their own boogeyman, and sent no return messages. So I remain on my own." She fought for a deep breath. "And now the diamonds."

Kieran York

Unwrapping the stones, Delbert inquired, "Why do you want them?"

"I've given my fortune to those who didn't shun me or ridicule me. My money is all going to those charities and causes accepting me and my people. Only to those causes. To my causes." She lined up the sparkling diamonds by size. They glimmered in their row. Behind them was a glass of water. "They say you can't take it with you. Perhaps you can take it partially away. These diamonds belong near me always. As the ancients would have taken their dearest possessions with them, I take mine. The diamonds represent a long line of fine love."

She lifted the first diamond chip and placed it between her chapped lips. Then she followed with the second. Soon she had swallowed the ninth. It was the three-carat given her by her final lover. She drank the remainder of water. With a feeble effort she put the empty glass down.

Delbert's smile lifted. "You will take them with you, my old girl." He pointed toward the two pills in a small paper cup. "And your medication." He poured a bit more water into her glass.

"Ah, yes. Placebos to wash the palate. To accompany my last supper. The final course."

"Adie," Delbert sifted words, "perhaps you're only being acquitted of life."

"Released. Perhaps, dear friend." Her lips lifted for a moment as her eyes blinked. "But it has all been so splendid." Her eyes watered slightly. "Splendid."

"Do you recall the time we went into the pool wearing our tuxedos?"

"And do you remember the time we went into the pool wearing our evening gowns?"

"Yes, my friend. Yes," he answered. The grip on her hand tightened. His eyes flooded. "I shall miss you."

"But not for long," she bantered.

"Not for long," he repeated. "Your life has been full. So why am I wishing for more? Is that selfish?"

"No." Her breathing became labored. "But I am satisfied. How wonderful - how very extraordinary. To have come to the end and be so satisfied with life's wonder."

"Do you remember your first fashion show in Paris?"

"No. *No.* I remember heaping mountains of black currant jam onto my mother's steaming muffins. There was a delft-blue and white jelly bowl." Her eyelids sagged, nearly covering her bronze eyes. She tipped the two pills into the palm of her hand. Sliding them between her lips, she swallowed. Suddenly, a brief, seemingly inextinguishable sheen lit her gaze. "I remember love."

BLUFF

Lorraine Warren knew that breakfast was becoming a worn rendition of bacon, eggs, toast, and the blues. She sat at the breakfast nook quietly. Across from a set of flatware, plates, and platters, sat her lover of ten years, Caroline Boyd. Their midlife crisis had seemed to continue through their thirties and was now approaching their fourth decade.

"You look at me as though you're waiting on me to make a difficult chess move," Caroline murmured. She then continued perusing several pages of a business report.

Nervously, Lorraine began humming a show tune. She halted suddenly, remembering how noise upset Caroline when she read. "Would you please pass the toast?"

Caroline slid the plate across the table. Finally Caroline glanced up. "You knew I'd be late last night. The red-eye special doesn't even leave until midnight. I suppose now you're going to threaten to split. We go through the same bullshit every time I can't account for a couple of hours."

"You mean every time you act out your sex-junkie nature. Then you pull out all of the mitigating circumstances," Lorraine accused. "Or shall we go for some cutesy euphemism. Every time you *misbehave.*" Lorraine took a bite of her toast. It was as tasteless as the rest of the meal. She chewed with anger. She stabbed the hash-browns with her fork. She then dropped her fork. The clatter made her blink. "Caroline, it isn't what I had in mind when we settled down. We're no longer happy."

"My suggestion is that you de-victimize. That might get you through the primrose path of life." With husky sigh Caroline pitched down her napkin. "We live in this grandiose, luxury home. Drive expensive cars. Wear designer threads." She hesitated, surveying the elegant, immaculate kitchen. "You've got to admit we're a pretty good team. We've got everything we want. Our yard is meticulously gardened, and our home is scrubbed clean for us. We have bucks to travel, go to the finest restaurants; do damn near everything we want. I warn you, if we break up, all this is going to be liquidated." Caroline resumed reading.

Lorraine balanced warm toast on her fingertips before taking a small bite. With an introspective clamp of her eyelids, she allowed her thoughts to drift. There was always such contempt in their dialogue. Silence escalated her anger. But why pursue a conversation. Their acidic intonation only calibrated with mutual contempt.

Both women knew the sessions by heart. Lorraine listed Caroline's multitude of infidelities. Caroline countered by accusing Lorraine of still being in love with her high school sweetheart. The love of Lorraine's life had been killed in an auto accident the year after they had come out together. Caroline's allegations stung Lorraine for more reasons than she cared to admit. That, Caroline contended, was the reason Lorraine held back so much of her love. Lorraine would then mention that if Caroline didn't blatantly cheat with a stable of tarts, she might be able to give her love more freely.

They knew the sequence as if they were scrolling through their brains. They were accomplices, building, growing, and fueling their dispute. They emptied round after round of venom at one another. Then, in separate vehicles, they drove to their work places. These, Lorraine believed, were the safe havens.

Lorraine realized that she wished she were at work. She slashed the icy silence with stern words. "You're correct. We have a great deal to lose. But maybe it's time we consider parting." She watched Caroline sip coffee. There was no hint of alarm. Caroline had heard it all before. She'd dealt with it all before. "Caroline, can you please put down your papers and listen to what I'm saying?"

Caroline's scowl targeted. "You want to go. Go. You want the entire lesbian community to know that I'm a worthless scamp, get a damned bullhorn and tell everyone what a loser I am. Fine. At least my tarts give me a little warmth."

"I'm past caring about your dalliances. You're indiscretions no longer even hurt me. Caroline, we're both young enough to begin again. I'm sure we each can meet someone else's needs. We might find someone special. Not only for cocktail parties. Remember the time you told me that the reason you were with me, besides the financial benefits of pooling our executive salaries, was that we made a cute couple?"

"That about sums it up."

"But we're not a contented couple."

"After a decade most couples aren't gregarious."

"But they aren't miserable."

"Lorraine, you think we should cut and run before our faces begin to line and our midsections begin to widen. Split before we're too dilapidated to find anyone else." She laughed a cruel, uncaring laugh meant to inflict sorrow. "Your chances of replacing me are limited. Your boobs might sag into yours stockings, so let's change partners fast."

"Our relationship is a failure. We're defeated." She glanced away. With honestly in her words, she spoke softly, "Caroline, the vows, hopes, and desires are gone. We're holding on to the familiar. Nothing else. We're economically dependent on two salaries to maintain our lifestyle. But as human beings, we're unfulfilled. We're emotional rubble."

"Rubble. Shit, Lorraine, that's part of your problem. Your damned liberal arts major makes you unfit for reality. You're back with turn-of-the century romance novels. You want to communicate, but it's impossible with you. We don't talk the same language. You expect a lesbian goddess to swoop out of the skies, pull you onto her steed, then together gallop off into the sunset. Together. Only a drama major could save you." Her arms flared back in a semicircle. Her eyes narrowed as she droned, "My darling, we are both screwed by this relationship. Reality doused the magic lantern."

"See how wrong we are together. You have no idea what I'm all about."

"Of course, I do." Caroline took a final sip of coffee.

"No." Lorraine collected her argument. "My words seem unreasonable to you."

"Because I'm a realist. I accept us."

Lorraine understood that the words were predestined - memorized. There was a blank patch between grimaces and flaring anger. There was space between desire and attainment. Now, even as desire was absent, truth was juggled. The killer named *desire* squared off with the killer *betrayal*. Each woman's image bank reran the script. They'd taken care to decorate their surroundings, but there were too many deadly images and poisonous words to ever imagine loving again.

Caroline bit hard when she slid the last square of bacon into her mouth. The crunch was solid, reflecting frustration. "Maybe," she offered, "a vacation might help. There was something compelling in her suggestion. Tragically so. It was seen by Lorraine. Caroline's suggestion was as charcoal gray as a storm's underside. Caroline was accomplished at retrieving Lorraine's hope.

Complicated, disturbing, and predictably sad, Lorraine considered, but true. Each time she studied the confrontations, she came to better know her vulnerability. She ultimately acquiesced. "Vacation time," she repeated. "I think this time *separate* vacations might be the only thing that helps."

"Separate vacations?" Caroline leaned nearer.

"Yes. I need time to think."

Caroline seemed genuinely stunned. "You need time to think about how rotten your life with me is? Lorraine, we're the envy of all the other couples we know. It would be a shame to end everything we have."

"We have our possessions."

"And we both love those possessions. We have both worked hard for them."

"But that isn't any longer enough. I want love. I want to laugh again. I want to feel as though I'm the most important person in the world to someone."

Caroline rubbed her forehead. "We're sharing our life together."

"It isn't enough. I no longer even feel passion for you."

Caroline dryly commented, "Every night you fall asleep on the sofa. Wild amorous sex is a thing of the past. No, I take that back. We never truly had that."

"At least you never had it with me." Lorraine covered her eyes. Her hand was a drape closing off brightness and the ache she felt.

"I understood early on that your dead ex-lover hauled you into the grave with her. And you expected me to be celibate while you romanced the ghost of your ex."

"If you'd given me time, I might have gotten over it. But you began your bed-hop." Lorraine glanced down at her empty coffee cup. A small leg of coffee streamed its side. "We can take vacations. I don't believe that's going to change my mind. At this point I'd rather have a small townhouse, drive an economy car, and mop my own floors."

"Lorraine, you're upset now. Tonight we'll go out to dinner."

"Was last night with your trick unworthy of another fling?"

Exasperated, Caroline looked away. "Better than nothing," Caroline confessed. "Look, can we call a truce until tonight. Someday one of us will say the words that are the final straw."

"I'm grasping at the final straw right now."

"The other women don't matter to me. They know they don't. I don't know why you don't know that."

Lorraine rinsed the dishes. She emptied the paper filter of coffee grounds. They splattered like freckled stars. Her eyes began to water. "I don't know how much they mean to you."

"Nothing. They mean nothing." Caroline's words were choppy. "I'm not sure I can make it without you. I've wanted to show you I'm as successful as your lost love would have been."

"That's the one thing I do know," Lorraine confirmed. "I suppose knowing that has been the only reason I've stayed with you. I've clung like a barnacle to some imaginary truss. I hoped love might happen. I'm equally guilty; equally needy."

"Lorraine, I'm sorry. I just want you to love me." Tears pressed from her eyes. Lorraine had never before assumed any responsibility. "Your love is all I've ever wanted. Don't you see, we've been all wrong. Times when I've tried, you haven't. Times when you've tried, I haven't. I give you my word that I'll continue trying – if you'll give us one more try. I am truly sorry."

"Perhaps after we return from vacation, we'll both be less sorry." She wasn't certain which woman's love she required. Lorraine glanced up at the expensive inset lighting. It showed no brightness on the tainted evidence of her pain.

"I'll settle for *perhaps*."

Lorraine had never see Caroline's tears accompany her promise. Lorraine repeated, "Perhaps."

CASTAWAY CREEK

Nineteen-hundred and eighty had begun without much fanfare. Not much changed - not much arranged. Castaway Creek had always been serenely wondrous. *Had* and *been* were the operative words. They were past-tense clues for the state of disarray that was part of the Castaway Creek landscape. Part that began recently. The peaceful nature was being disrupted. Jesse Bonner was damned if she'd allow that to happen to her beloved mountain town.

Nestled back a ways in the Colorado Rocky Mountains is a dot-on-the-map community called Castaway Creek. Barely a town, the population is right around five-hundred folks. Three-hundred year-round residents, actually. Eighty percent, Jesse 'sposed, were lesbian. If the latest estimates are anything to go by, that is. Drawing the circle wider, many women decided on the area, but lived out a bit - although still in the county.

Jesse referred to weekenders as the *sunshine* people. They were folks coming to their cabins to fish Castaway Creek. They might make it up on a winter weekend or two. They might snowshoe, cross-country ski, or just get away from their city lives.

Castaway was a neighborhood of scattered cabins strung together by a gravel road. That trail met centrally at the Castaway Bar and Grill. Next to the bar was the Castaway Trading Post. Jesse and her lover of over twenty-five years, Mara Kerr, had purchased the Trading Post a decade ago. When the rustic little general store and gas station had been placed on the market, Jesse and Mara purchased it straight away. It seemed predestined. Not only was it directly across from their own small cabin, but they had decided this is where they belonged.

They never once regretted buying the Trading Post. Relocating permanently to Castaway was the best thing that ever happened. They renovated the shabby, little general store some. For if Castaway Creek was the heart of Sapphic mountain living - Jesse and Mara had become the heartbeats.

However, it was their twelve-year old calico cat named Dottie that become Castaway Creek's first and only mayor. Left in Dottie's capable paws, the township stayed exactly the same, year after year. Jesse bragged that this was as it should be. Dottie knew the best way to govern: keep your whiskers clean, your belly filled, and your litter-box tidy. The remainder of administrative duties weren't important. After all, give the people what they want. And the vote had been a landslide in Dottie's favor.

Both Jesse and Mara were approaching sixty. Between happiness, staying active with outdoor recreation, and their never-ending stocking of the general store, they felt years younger. Mara claimed the crisp mountain air kept them vigorous. Jesse believed that folks create their own victory. And tranquility, she stressed, was the key to their well-being.

At least, Castaway Creek had been a restful, stress-free respite.

Three years ago the Castaway Bar and Grill was purchased by their dear friend, Ruthie Starr. Now, Ruthie was not the problem. She'd always maintained peace. Then, a year ago, she hired a transient woman to work in her bar. Ruthie had made what she considered a terrific find.

Constance Fraser was not only an excellent bartender, but she also entertained some on weekends. She played guitar and sang like an angel. Con, as she preferred to be called, was also competent at fixing anything that wasn't in proper working order. She called herself a hell of a handywoman.

Mara commented she must have been very *handy* indeed. Ruthie and Con became lovers. To Jesse's dismay. Con Fraser was not up to Jesse's measurement for becoming Ruthie's spouse. Ruthie's generous, easygoing nature should have the proper accompaniment. She deserved a woman of substance; a woman who met with Jesse's approval. Not an easy thing to do.

Con was no such woman. She was surly, snarly, and her biting sarcasm often was on the edge of being cruel. There's where the tension began. Jesse and Mara knew that Ruthie was impressed with Con's musical talents. But the strange interloper was also downright moody and difficult. Especially when she imbibed. Then her gloom truly intensified.

There was more. Con was secretive about her past. She'd shut down a prying conversation in a blink. Just ahead of the posse, Con changed subjects, stormed out of the room, or often clammed up. She was nearing forty-years of age, but it was as if those first decades hadn't existed. After a confrontation, assuredly, she set out to consume as much booze as she was able, before Ruthie intervened.

Last night another battle had taken place between Ruthie and Con. Jesse's grin was extinguished when she heard a ruckus begin across the street. "What you 'spose that's about?" Mara questioned.

"Con is making a problem of herself," Jesse replied with a soft mumble. She finished the final rim of pie crust that was on her plate. She didn't mind eating right before going to bed. With the ruckus across the street, she figured she wouldn't get too much sleep early on anyway. Why not add a dose of heartburn to it all?

* * *

"Now, Jesse, we mustn't get involved."

The Castaway Trading Post was becoming lit with the tawny sunshine that spilled in nearly every morning.

"Involved! *Involved!* Ruthie is like a daughter to us," Jesse stormed. "By damn, they sounded like a couple of wild cats 'til way after two this morning and you don't want to get involved. My sleep, or lack of it, is plenty involved. We have to open up here early and I'm not rested. Hell, it's getting colder now and that doesn't improve my mood. Autumn's cool mornings are closing in. Makes me feel like I haven't had any sleep at all."

"You're ranting," Mara indicted.

"I'm not. I'm concerned for Ruthie."

"Last night's commotion is best left to Ruthie to sort." Mara stuffed another few chunks of coal into the potbellied stove. "This will be fired up in no time. Rest of the day will be nice and toasty for you. I promise. And Ruthie hasn't asked for help in sorting her troubles. So we'd best leave it to them."

"She's ass-over-teakettle in love with Con. And that Con is a misery from the ground up."

Mara's sigh was explosive. "Now stop your conniption fit. Ruthie will be fine."

"Doesn't sound like it. She's not doing her own sorting." They exchanged significant glances. Jesse sulked as she peeped between the narrow blinds. Con's battered red pickup truck was parked off to the side of the bar. Around the truck's perimeter a half dozen empty beer bottles were scattered. "A circle of empties points in the direction of Con sleeping in her truck last night."

"It may have been from earlier on."

"It might have been from that pesky squirrel out there sucking up suds and pitching empty beer bottles. Damn squirrel is big enough to put a saddle on. Keeps foraging from the bird's feeder."

"Then we should make a little ledge with dried corn and nuts for the squirrel. Besides, those little birds are pretty good at fending for themselves. But we'll double up on the seed come winter. They'll all be fine. And so will Ruthie."

Mara's broom preened the oak floor. She was dressed in denims, dark blue full-length apron that covering the front of her turtleneck sweater, and high hiking boots. Mara's thin figure skimmed the room. Long silver-gray hair was pulled back and tied away from her naturally glowing face. Pale blue eyes flashed with energy and enthusiasm.

Jesse had fallen in love with those penetrating eyes nearly forty years ago. But Mara was with another woman. Jesse backed away. After years of sad affairs on both sides, the women met again. This time love was to be. They settled down and for the last two and a half decades, shared love.

Both women had aged gracefully. Jesse's short, wavy dark hair was now heavily salted with gray. Her face had become more squared, more defined, with age. Her bright hazel eyes and her teasing smile had captivated Mara. Her form had become slightly stocky - more sturdy. She hid her expanding midsection by wearing bulky plaid shirts with their tails hanging out over her denims. And it was more comfy.

Their quietude was relevant. It translated to mean that Mara needed a moment to consider the situation. Mara joined Jesse at the window. "I don't believe they ever had such a row. But I still say we need to stay well out of it."

"Ruthie's history with women isn't the best. Picks needy women. Most of them open their mouths and lies flow out. She buys into every blasted one of those lies. Eats them like good candy."

"Well, Con hasn't lied to her."

"Con doesn't tell her a damn thing about her past. For all we know, she's an ax murderer."

"What are you going on about?" Mara questioned with amusement.

"Ruthie's love is like a runaway horse where Con's concerned. I don't understand it." Jesse frowned. "We should do something."

"Just because she's like a daughter to us doesn't mean we have a right to say anything. Ruthie is a joy. I don't want her getting all aggravated at us. She's sunshine in our lives. We chance losing her friendship if we interfere."

Jesse smiled. "She's too trusting and good-natured." Sunshine. Yes, Jesse considered. Ruthie has the ability to make everyone around her happy. Her long, curly blonde hair constantly sways. Her sparkling cornflower-blue eyes dazzle her clientele. A milk-white smile flashes from her tawny peach complexion. Lovely in her tight denims, bright western shirts, and flowered scarves, she is. She reminded Jesse of springtime. Perhaps it was her lilac dusting powder. But even in winter's core, Ruthie exudes warmth and brightness. Her family, back in Wyoming, was upset when Ruthie decided to move. Castaway Creek didn't sound like her kind of place. A woman shouldn't be hidden away in a small mountain community. But Ruthie found her home in Castaway.

"She's in love. Well, maybe not last night," Mara conceded. "But she actually sees something in Con."

Con was a total contrast to Ruthie. Jesse deliberated. Her sigh gushed. Even Con's tall, steep slenderness moved with a somber plod. Ebony eyes sulked from her ivory skin. Eyes seemed a perfect match with her mid-length dark hair. Con dressed mostly in western-wear, but sometimes interspersed denim with khaki.

Strangely incongruous was her lack of feelings. The only time she showed the range of her passion was when she sang her songs. Even the sad ones made her animated with an inner emotion displayed only with her guitar in hand.

"Mara, how can anyone be around Ruthie, share Ruthie's blossomy bed, and be so sour? Except when Con's on stage, you'd think she's in a pit digging away at life."

Mara laughed. "Ever notice when Con picks up her guitar, she holds it so tightly you'd think it was her last friend. Her only friend."

By the time the set of songs was completed, Con's face became chiseled in pain. Her gravelly, whiskey voice was so lonely, it groped at mellow lyrics.

While Con and Jesse had never exchanged angry words, there was a hidden disclaimer. The battle lines were drawn. Con was never accepted. She realized that. The first time they'd met Con, she asked if Castaway was named for societal castaways. Jesse was not amused. With reined anger, Jesse answered that her town was named because of the abundance of cutthroat and rainbow trout. Anyone fishing the banks of the many small lakes and streams could castaway their angling lines and fill their limit by noon.

Jesse was fiercely proud of Castaway Creek. No place like it, she contended. The smoky, tame river appeared to be cascading diamonds when the sun beamed on it. In winter, the river sent streams of rushing, glinting white caps above the ice. Icicles hung over craggy rocks and were framed by downy snow. Great spruce trees, in the distance, were like nature's sentinels. The scene became a hand-stenciled postcard from the creator, Jesse often said. There was no season Jesse did not love.

She did not love, however, the cutting remarks issued by Con about Castaway. Nor could she tolerate Con's verbal jabs about the folks. Mara always tried to defend Con's biting words. Well, maybe Con didn't mean it that way, she defended. Always, Jesse ruminated, Mara looked for the good.

She brought up the fact that Con *was* accepted by animals of Castaway Creek. She was always patching up one animal or another. Mayor Dottie often found the best spot for her official duties was in Con's lap. And Con was devoted to Ruthie's old dog, Geronimo. Geronimo's mixed breed included wolf and shepherd. It made him a natural for his elected office as town chief-of-police.

"I know," Jesse blurted. "And any minute now you're going to bring up Con's saving grace. She loves animals. And they take to her."

"Got to admit, that is a lovely trait."

Jesse wrapped her arms around Mara. Her kiss brushed against her lover's forehead. "After they bickered, Ruthie must have finally had it. Kicked her out."

"Not a bunch irks our Ruthie. But she must have been angry. Probably relented and went out to haul Con home before it got too nippy." Mara's word pretended optimism.

"If not, Con's probably mighty cold."

Mara suggested, "Think you should go out to check on her?"

Jesse chuckled. "What shall I ask her? Con, I see you're not in the bosom of your goddess. Need a heart to heart?"

"Now you stop that!" Mara's smile escaped. "Try to be a friend to her," Mara encouraged.

"Maybe I should approach the truck by throwing red meat into her cage first."

"You can be an old coot when you set your mind to it," Mara teased. She pressed nearer the window. "Looks like you won't need to bother. Ruthie's on her way out."

The women watched Ruthie exit the bar. She headed directly

toward the Trading Post. "Not even stopping by Con's truck. Must want to let her sleep it off. It's obvious it didn't rain empties out there, so she's got to know where Con is."

The brass bell above the door jingled. Ruthie entered. The soles of her western boots slapped the floorboards. She examined Jesse's scowl. "Now, Jesse, keep your powder dry. We'll have everything patched up by noon," Ruthie announced. "And we'll get the area cleaned up."

"Ruthie, why take all this aggravation?" Jesse questioned. "You could do better."

"For me there is no better. I love Con."

"You're asking for a world of hurt."

"Jesse," Ruthie began, "I can't explain it." She turned, looking at the wall. After many seconds of intermission, her glance redirected to Jesse. "You don't know her."

"What I know is that she's dead drunk out there in the bed of her pickup. What I know is that she gave you troubles last night. My hearing is still strong." Jesse's side-glance in Mara's direction told her of Mara's disapproval. "Okay. I won't say more."

"You don't need to take a loyalty oath," Ruthie joked. "I know you mean well." She leaned back against the knotty pine counter. "And you needn't remind me that you're my designated protector. As long as you're on my side."

Jesse nodded. "Always on your side." Her brow cuffed into an intense frown. She attempted to ease the taut moment. "For all this bother, is she that great in the sack?"

Ruthie smiled. "Lovemaking is always tender. Like when her voice moans a love song. She can be the most tender I've ever known. Sometimes her kiss is my life. She's for me. But there is something in her that's untamed."

"You believe she's for you?"

"Jesse, I know I'm for her. Under it all, she's the most frightened person I've ever met. Sometimes she's terrified." A stampede of emotion rushed across Ruthie's face. She gazed out the window toward the battered truck. "Terrified."

Jesse reached for Ruthie's shoulder. "I know you're the strong one in this relationship. But what do you get back?"

Ruthie's eyes became mildewy. "At one time in her life she stopped loving. Then she forgot how. She needs to learn it all again. She needs time. She needs friends, too."

"I'm not sure she wants my friendship. She's got a funny way of showing it if she does."

"Jesse, all love begins with trust. She needs to trust enough not to be frightened of giving love. If she loses love again, I don't think she could take it. She's trapped by fear."

"Trapped, hell," Jesse disputed. "She's in hanky-panky heaven. Has a place to stay over the bar. Gets to share your bed. And she's cry-babying about love? She's got a good woman to love her. That's not trapped."

"Jesse," Ruthie requested, "why don't you get her in for me?"

"Why me?" Jesse quizzed with a wounded expression. "I like her least of anyone here."

"Please. For me, try?"

Jesse pulled on her jacket vest. She snapped it shut with urgency. "I'll try to talk some sense into her."

"No, Jesse. Her world doesn't make sense now. Ask her to be your friend."

* * *

Jesse ambled to the truck. She constructed words of wisdom. When she got to the truck's edge she heard a groan. With her foot on the bumper, Jesse swung her body upward. Once in the pickup's bed, she stared down at Con.

Con was curled into a fetal hug. Her hat, with rattlesnake-skin band, dipped over her face. Jesse nudged Con's shoulder. With a start, Con's body lurched. She shrieked. Her voice strained. When her eyes flew open, Jesse saw stark terror. Not the terror of a bad dream, but horror-stricken fear. It was the alarm of fearing for one's very life.

"Ruthie sent me to fetch you."

Con swallowed away a knot in her throat before she spoke. "Ruthie must really be pissed if she sent you." She reached for a bottle of whiskey that was at her side. Uncapping it with a vengeance, Con put the rim to her mouth. The swig was long and desperate. Her eyes batted as the fumes rose. She appeared to be roping herself back to reality. She stammered, "Or was it your idea to come out here so you can tell me what a shit I am?"

"I'm not here to scold you. You wouldn't listen anyway. If you want to toss a good woman's love away with both hands, it's up to you. We hate to see Ruthie hurt. But she loves you." Jesse shrugged as she studied Con's facial contortions.

"I love her." Con propped her body up against the back of the cab.

"Just between us, why are you drinking so heavy? Trying to forget something or someone?"

"I want to forget everything and everyone before Ruthie."

"Helps drinking, does it?"

"That's right. It helps." She held up the nearly drained bottle. "This is my sanity."

Her eyes were hard-chipped. They combined hurt with hate.

"I know you think I can nag the bark off a tree, but I'm only going to be telling you this once. Ruthie may put up with your damned moodiness. She may take your bad humor. But she's not going to be able to watch you hang your liver out to dry every morning after a toot."

"Booze helps me sleep."

"The hell. You two fought most of the night. How did that help?"

Con's eyes were blank, enameled. "Just leave it." Her words were drolly spoken. She returned to a vacuous stare as silence lingered.

"You're going to lose Ruthie if you keep this up. You're feeling sorry for yourself. Think about her once."

"I try."

"Con, why is your past life such a forbidden subject?"

"It's painful."

"And your past is why you can't sleep without drinking?"

"I guess." Con's body pressed back. Her eyes narrowed. Tormented, they then clamped shut. She was lost in a thread of memory and alcoholic stupor. "Did you know that some starlight comes from collapsed stars?"

"Con, tell me about your past." Jesse sensed abandonment. She reached to touch Con's leg. "You know me well enough to know that I'd never betray a confidence. So tell me. Everyone has pain along the way. That's part of life. Tell me about yours."

Con slowly opened her eyes. A line, a lens of tears, filled her eyes, then flooded them. Her mouth slowly moved as if it were thawing. Slowly, words began to sneak out. "A decade and a half ago I was a nurse in Nam. The carnage twisted my heart until it died." She flinched. "I came home believing I'd be able to stop counting bodies. Stop seeing the gush of blood everywhere. Limbs torn. Burnt bodies.

Aw, shit," she broke. "I tried to return to living. I didn't make it. I ended up addicted. Another fresh start. Then another one. Finally I beat hard drugs. Replaced them with booze. It's legal anyway." Her eyes dimmed. "Every time I dry up, I realize there's no reason for me to clean up. I'm still living inside this fucking nightmare."

"Ruthie is a reason for you to sober up."

Tears unlocked and began to pour down her face. Con leaned against the outstretched arms of Jesse. "I'm so frightened she's going to see through me. See how my heart has been strangled. See the real sick me. She deserves to be with someone who can love her. Someone complete. I'm incomplete."

"That woman in there loves you. In your past, you gave the best skills you had to heal others. Healing your own pain isn't impossible. You've got Ruthie. We each invent our own optimism. You can survive."

"You know how many soldiers died in my arms. They wanted to survive. They wanted me to help them. I couldn't help them all."

"You did the best you could for them. You risked your life to save theirs. It isn't your fault if you couldn't save them all."

"It wasn't their lucky day? They gasped for breath. Their eyes pleaded. They fought for life. Luck is seasonal."

"Women like Ruthie aren't seasonal."

"Don't you understand, every time I give myself totally, I still lose. I held together until I reached stateside. Then I was empty. Empty. But I tried." Stranded, remote, Con's eyes shut. "Sometimes when Ruthie holds me, it's almost like I'm safe again."

Jesse squeezed Con to her. She felt the woman's sobs bubbling up, uncontrollable. "Being safe is often being loved. It's a start. And if you can beat drug addiction, you can beat booze. And if you have the love of a good woman, you *can* do anything."

Con's smile lifted. "I do adore her."

"Then talk out your memories. You've hidden them away too long. Truth revises itself. Time is forgiving. You've got to keep the dialogue going so Ruthie knows where you hurt."

"It's going to be difficult to tell people about."

Jesse nodded. "I always wondered how you knew about patching up the animals. A nurse, huh?"

"An ex-nurse."

"I'm not sure that there is such a thing as an ex-nurse." Jesse watched Con's eyes begin to withdraw from the conversation. "Listen to me - you've got to tell Ruthie. She can help."

"Like I said, it's tough to talk about. Maybe it's hardest to talk about with the person I love. I don't want her to be hurt."

"You just told me." Jesse's hands cupped the younger woman's cheeks. "Now I'll tell you something. I'm frightened, too. I'm afraid I might not be able to be a good enough friend to help you. But I'm not going to let that fear stop me from trying." She felt Con's body tremble.

"What if I'm too lost to make it?"

"I don't believe you are. Ruthie doesn't believe you are." Jesse smiled. "Besides, we're in a place where winning is just another recreational sport. We are the women of Castaway Creek."

"What if I can't get it together?" Her pain was reaching out. It was grasping, and it was pleading. "What if *I* lose?"

Jesse realized what Con meant when she said that some starlight comes from collapsed stars. "Now," she offered, "if you lose, we'll all lose."

Photograph by Kathie Solie

DAINTY TWININGS

Once upon a time there existed an enchanted Elfin Colony called Elm Village. Deep in the heart of a verdant, forest meadow of Timber Valley, Elm Village was located. The hollowed Elm Tree residents numbered over two-hundred Elves. All of Timber Valley, including Fir Junction, Birch Basin, and Cottonwood Gulch, was ruled by duel deities: Mother Earth and Father Time.

Elm Village was the home tree of Mecha. She was a lovely little Elf facing one of the most difficult dilemmas known in Elf dome. She was now of age. According to Elfin ritual, she was to select her life mate. Once selected, their nuptials would be forever held and honored. The Elves pledged themselves to be twined as one - for all time. The binding of their hearts made their heartbeat become one. Forever and always that beat was in perfect unison. If they ever parted, each Elf possessed only half a heart.

Because the decision was of the greatest importance, Mecha anguished over her crucial determination. Complications were many. Throughout her life, Mecha had always taken problems to her grandmother, Gamba. Gamba offered guidance and wisdom to her lovely young Elfin granddaughter. For Gamba had been through her own youth. She knew that the Time an Elf spends *is* life. For that reason, each moment is to be treated with reverence and love. Gamba knew that problems are little more than Life Puzzles. This she had often told Mecha.

Mecha entered the tree trunk hollows. With weighty steps, she made her way up to her grandmother's seventh branch cubbyhole apartment. Her enlarged, tent-shaped eyes blinked as she accustomed them to the dimness. She was a replicated version of her grandmother. Naturally, she possessed the same dimples in her apple cheeks. And the glint beaming from her eyes was a younger version of Gamba's. Now, Gamba's silky hair had turned from golden to a silver meringue billows atop her head.

The diminutive old Elf invited her granddaughter inside. "Mecha, I view your heart. You are greatly troubled."

Mecha knew of Gamba's magical powers. Gamba allowed Mecha a moment to see inside herself, if she wished. Mecha explained, "It's my nuptials." She sat across from her grandmother on a soft mushroom stool's pillow. "Gamba, there are two Elves I dearly love. I divide my favors. Both are good; both are kind."

"Better two than none," Gamba gently chided. She fidgeted with a moss lace doily. "And your heart is uncertain?"

"It seems so complicated. There is Tad. And there is my dear friend, Lela."

"The deities are great and glorious. They have provided us with the power of making selections that are best for our own being. For we have Nature's programming. We must always listen first to our hearts."

"I want to make the proper decision."

"It is made within you. But let the nobility of purpose assist you in becoming your own potential. It is only up to the heart. So tell me, Mecha, which of your suitors is best for you?"

"Tad is a fine tribute to Elfhood. He is a good friend."

"Yes. And he is handsome. His ears are very big indeed. His adornment is seldom ruffled. And although he is mischievous, he is never cruel. He makes everyone laugh."

"He is playful," Mecha said with an impish grin. "As is Lela." She thought about their frolic. The three of them scampered through the woods with total abandon. "Yes, they are the cause of my gladness in sunshine."

"If you select Lela over Tad, there can be no reproduction. The twining with another female Elf excludes Elflets."

"But there is a woeful overpopulation. There is barely enough vacant trees to accommodate our many tree trunk villages."

"It will come down to where you best belong. Mecha, for many seasons I believed Tad and your other friend, Riva, might twine."

Mecha glanced away. "She also dearly loves Tad. But she told me that it is my choice, as I have come of age first. Riva said she also knows I care for Lela. And Riva is not ready for twining yet, but I know that Tad would wait for her, if I do not select him. She is young, and not a serious Elf."

"She will not be angry if you select Tad?"

"No. Riva wants my happiness. And she believes that one day in Time, she will find her heart's path."

"She realizes that each Elf has many different Natures. But we all have the exact same hearts."

"Gamba, there is only the path of one's heart. It's the way Elves work."

"Exactly," Gamba agreed. "There is no job description to being an Elf. Other than kindness and fun."

"Both Lela and Tad are kind and fun. They are excellent at bareback-frog hopping rodeos. And each can play many melodies on bluebells."

With charm, Gamba nodded. "Both are very fine. Your decision will be the correct one. We shall welcome either of them into our family tree. And proudly so." With serenity, she added, "And Mecha, our Natures are never false. They give true messages. We must all recognize what we are. If your feelings for Lela are true, it is your best Nature. If your feelings for Tad are true, it is also your best Nature. Your little Elfin eyes will beam for her or for him. And your little Elfin heart will set off chimes. The song of truth will sing for you. There is in each of us a tiny space within our hearts that listens in on romance."

* * *

Warm summer rains had produced a sandalwood scent throughout the woods. Mecha, Lela, Tad, and Riva frolicked most of the day. They then hid in a mint field beneath rose petal shelters until the rains melted away to mist.

With great decorum, they scampered to the strawberry pavilion. It was Mecha's favorite place to play. She waited for the beam of love to radiate from her eyes. She listened closely to her heart messages. Her search for the delicate twine of romance was not pressing, but a patient suspension was with her. Chiming was its own magic, she knew.

Riva and Lela began a game of tug with the stem of an oak leaf. Mecha whispered her feelings to Tad. "You are a fine Elf, Tad. And my dear friend, as well. My decision will be best for both of us."

"If you want Lela, I understand. She is very fetching in her lovely colors of ruby and poppy-yellow. Her outfits are always as if the rainbow had wrapped her. Look how the clouds puffed up and took the rains away," he chattered.

"Do you like Riva?"

"Mecha, there is an Elf for every other Elf. Of course I like Riva."

Then he scurried off to chase after Riva and Lela.

Mecha's pansy-shaped face fell into her hands. The moment was tranquil, but puzzling. Then without hesitation, she glanced up. She saw Lela's happy, shining face. Their eyes bridged. Mecha stood. She rushed across the forest floor. Her legs raced toward Lela. When she reached Lela's side, her voice froze. She attempted to read Lela's eyebeams with accuracy. Remembering that she had brought a pocket full of Elfin gumdrops, Mecha reached into her pocket. She pulled out a lavender candy. Her hand opened as she extended her offering. "For you, Lela."

Lela's radiant smile was luminous. She poked the gumdrop into her mouth and chewed for many moments. Then she frowned.

"What is wrong?" Mecha questioned.

"That's very strange."

"What is strange, Lela?"

"My heart is playing a melody."

"And?"

"Mecha, your eyes are very bright with beams. Are you listening? Do you hear the magical chimes?"

"Yes. Yes, Lela." Her smile bloomed across her face. Mecha was the most joyous Elf in all of Elm Village. In fact, all of Timber Valley. She thanked Mother Earth and Father Time for bestowing such wonder. Such a blessing. "Yes," she repeated. "Lela, I hear the music. It is our romance."

All the Elves lived Naturally ever after. Mecha believed that the legends about Elf's large ears must be correct. The better to listen to romance.

DOUBLE FAULTS

Once in the semifinals, Darcy no longer considered tennis a pastime. Although her court shenanigans didn't cease, she did get down to business. The seasoned champion, Darcy Lovett, was challenged by games on the court, as well as the game of courting. With either sport, she was always there to win.

This match was different. She had more riding on it. Although it was only a small invitational, with a small purse, she had sweetened the pot. When the twenty-year old lesbian realized she was to play the beautiful Julia Tully in the semi-final match, a challenge was issued.

Julia's sheltered eighteen years had not prepared her for Darcy's deal. Darcy had been chasing Julia for the entire summer, without results. And Darcy was used to being pursued by a bevy of lovely, young women. Julia wouldn't give her the time of day. Or night.

When Julia bragged that the match was hers, she boxed herself into a corner. She was then confident enough, or foolish enough, to wager on her win. Confidence, she'd been schooled, is a good thing, even when playing a higher ranked competitor. And her game had improved since she was last shut out by the flashy Darcy. So why not take the bet?

If Darcy lost, she agreed to cease her seduction efforts. She would never again invite Julia on a trip to Lesbos with her. But, should Julia lose, Darcy would be allowed to escort Julia on that journey.

Their rivalry had been in earnest before. And it was to be much more so now. Darcy, with her playful trot across the court, and her wild antics, was attempting to win over Julia's mechanized style.

"Can't you be quiet?" Julia shouted when Darcy whooped after winning the point. Julia pushed her strawberry blonde hair back. It was bundled into a long cord behind her back. It swayed with her as she rocked on the baseline. Delicate, her face was filled with a dusting of light freckles. Her hazel eyes blinked rapidly when she became serious. Her trim figure swayed, and her feet peddled in anticipation of Darcy's serve.

Darcy's muscular body seemed to perform magic with little

effort. She *played* at the game. When the line judge reprimanded her, she used a fluty mimicking voice to taunt her. Humor was license to accost the officials. And accost them she did. She'd shake her short, curly brown hair, and then whirl around pretending to fly. Her arms flapped wildly for many moments before she returned to finish her argument with the official. Her fawn-brown eyes, with their amber glints, provoked, and still humored. But when she flashed her paper-white smile, after the confrontation, she charmed them.

Julia won the second set, thankfully. The fact that they were both tough competitors was evidenced by the game. The sets were split down the middle: Six-four. Four-six. The third and deciding set was about to be played.

At the sideline, Darcy wiped her racket. "You're playing better than ever. No wonder you made it to the semifinals. You've really improved since we last played."

"I'll make it to the finals, too."

"Only if you beat me. And you wouldn't want to deprive me of collecting my prize," Darcy stressed her words. Her eyebrows teasingly shot up as she grinned.

Julia's eyes blazed. "Face it, I've not only improved my tennis, but I've also grown up. You don't intimidate me. And I'm surely not about to fall under your spell. Playgirls don't interest me."

"I'm not as much of a playgirl as you might think."

"Sure you are."

"I wouldn't mind settling down. Not if it's with you."

"I'm not interested in your lines."

Darcy improvised a shrug. "Well, here we go. Let's see what you've got. Make like Zorro, get in there, make our Zs and get out. Winner takes all. And I mean *all*. I can't wait to get you in the shower room after my win."

"Darcy, you may impress some women with your showbiz style, but not me."

"Whew!" Darcy suddenly became serious. "I'll let you in on a little secret. If I ever found a woman who is impressed with just me, not my racket, I'd settle down in a hurry. By the way, what color bed linens do you prefer?"

Julia's rancor was like a smashing fist. "Don't get your hopes up. In case you haven't looked at the scoreboard, we're in a tie."

"I wouldn't mind being tied to you for the next several decades."

Julia's confrontational voice seethed, "I plan to do battle this set. So don't throw away your telephone directory filled with sweethearts."

"For you I'd make that ultimate sacrifice."

"Prepare for defeat." Julia stood, tossed her towel, and with total determination, walked onto the court.

Darcy believed Julia. Her first serve was a cannonball ace. Julia's blistering backhand had also come alive. As the younger woman stutter-stepped at the baseline, it was more like a war dance.

When the line judge made what Darcy considered a bad call, she went into *showtime* mode. "Say it isn't so," she yelled as she hoisted her racket into the air. Catching it, she gave an elaborate bow in Julia's direction.

"Cut the bull and play," Julia yelled.

The next game was filled with a cross fire of volleys. Julia glared, smashed the ball with a vengeance, and then ignored Darcy. She was also winning. She seemed rejuvenated after switching sides. The women passed by the net, sharing a scowl.

"You're a powerhouse today," Darcy whispered.

"I don't want to lose."

Darcy towel-dried her moist face. She lamented, "I'm not as bad as you think. Lots of the talk is just publicity. I don't date *every* starlet in Hollywood." Her eyes became serene. "Julia, we can call it off. I promise never to bother you again. I see by your resolve that you really don't want to be with me."

"I don't renege on my challenges," Julia said curtly. "As promised, if you win, I'll be the best one-night stand you've ever had."

"That's what I'm trying to say. You're not the kind of woman I'd want to just have a fling with."

"Well don't count on even that. I'm going to win," she boasted.

"Bring it on," Darcy chided with a three-quarter grin. "The deal is still on."

"And I'm still winning."

After another hard-fought game, Darcy called over the net, "Even!"

On the next game, Julia played to advantage. Her backhand then sliced as she returned the ball into the net. As play continued, Darcy considered that it never seemed to take long to win, but it takes forever to lose. Just as Julia began rallying, her serve seemed to come apart. Advantage Darcy. Then Darcy's game stumbled. She began making errors. Advantage Julia Tully.

Finally there was game, set, and match. Darcy was victorious. She had held serve, won the match, and now was angry. She was galled that she hadn't thrown the match as she'd planned to do, allowing Julia off the hook. A swarm of fans followed her. Her ritual of flirting with them was no longer important.

By the time she reached the shower room, Darcy heard the drizzling water. Julia was inside the shower stall. Darcy undressed. She passed by Julia's stall. As she did, the door flipped open, steam poured out, and behind the mist she saw Julia's nudity. The young woman's eyes invited.

Darcy stepped nearer the cubical. "Julia, you don't need to do this."

She felt the clasp of Julia's arm pulling her under the raining waters. Her words of protest were hushed by Julia's kiss. Inside the buckle of Julia's embrace, Darcy felt the nearness of Julia. She'd never felt another woman's heartbeat. She'd always been too interested in their mutual orgasms.

Darcy confessed, "I wanted to throw the match."

Julia responded, "But I *did* throw the match. I didn't want to be just one more fan pursuing you."

Darcy leaned back. She looked longingly into Julia's face. "You care more about me than advancing your own career."

"Yes. I always have. But I never wanted a quick affair. I wanted *you*."

"You've got me." Darcy's eyes watered. "You could use some help to improve your serve."

"Are you offering to coach me?" Julie grinned.

"Yes, but I'm not much of a coach. It could take a while. Fifty or sixty years."

"You've got a deal, Darcy Lovett."

"My *second* win of the day."

EXPAT'S ANTHEM

September 11, 2001

The last ten months had given Captain Cory Daniels very little information about her lover, Gabrielle Moffatt. It had been the most exasperating, yet exhilarating time of Cory's life. It had been fine china. It had been paper plates. The forty weeks were hidden tears and they were tea-roses.

In a scant paragraph, Cory could recount Gabrielle's fact sheet. Gabrielle was an American expatriate living in a squalid pension on one of East London's side streets. She covered her sinewy eight-stone figure with denim, corduroy, and billowy poet's shirts. Like a bracelet, she wore a symbolically decorated handcuff on her right wrist. Upon first meeting Gabrielle, she quickly explained that the cuff did not express a penchant for S&M, but rather a statement against oppression. With great acrimony, she'd announced that her tyrannical former homeland, The United States of America, was her sworn enemy.

Cory's first glimpse of Gabrielle was yet remembered. There had been intrigue. She wondered if her fellow American was genuine. But quickly she found that Gabrielle's words were punched with venom. Gab's nerves were tightly wound. When discussing the topic, Gabs body motion was that of someone in a duel. Elegant, yet poised for attack, the Expat's anthem was a stinging dissertations.

With great irony Cory realized that Gab's appearance was soft. Shoulder-length, spice-colored hair was highlighted with flecks of yellow gold. Her pistachio-green eyes converted from flirt to flint in a millisecond. Inviting, somber, Gabrielle had seduced Cory's heart with a glance that was backed up by a mystical smile.

Gabrielle could be a tender lover - attentive and generous. She could make Cory feel as though she was the only women in the universe. Then Gabrielle might become lost within some far-off territory of her mind. As if fine-tuning her perception, Gab's thoughts took her on a hidden escape within. She denied being away - withdrawn. And her behavior became that of a sulking two-year old, rather than the demure, intelligent thirty-year old she actually was.

Gab was rich with the wisdom of an ancient sage. Yet she was also mystified by the mechanics of a modern age. She'd mastered the complexity of computer science, and carried with her a cutting-edge notebook. Yet, she elected to write her poetry on an antiquated Corona Special model produced by L.C. Smith and Corona Typewriter, vintage 1920s. The small, red, folding machine went from her desk to her nightstand and was always loaded with a sheet of blank typing paper. Gabrielle ate shepherd's pie and drank brown ale. And she was the saddest person Cory had ever known.

When Cory attempted to delve deeper, Gabrielle playfully questioned if Cory was doing an in-depth background search. She then broodingly answered Cory's inquiry by saying that nothing in her past mattered. Cory realized that it did matter. There was a bounty of solitude that created a wilderness of wounds. And they were not superficial. She saw a *long ago* hurt in Gab's eyes. One night, after a multitude of questions, Gab extracted a vow. There was to be no more probing her history.

Cory willingly made that vow. And inside, she was certain she could indeed rein her curiosity. She was a disciplined officer in the military. Her job, and her life, depended on a mandatory control. She was stationed in Germany, but would soon be deployed to the Middle East. Not only were her orders sacredly sealed, but there was also the 'no-ask/no-tell' proposition with which to contend. Confidentiality was assured, she told Gab when agreeing to the no-pry vow. Both women were afforded safety by respecting one another's privacy. Cory was fine with that - at first.

The second part of their initial vow was that neither woman would make an attempt to change one another's beliefs. Cory interpreted that to mean she was to make no attempt to persuade Gab to dispense with her credo of anti-Americanism. Cory was not to be attacked about her military allegiance. Cory, however, saw mistrust and hatred in her lover's eyes each time her native country was mentioned. The same country Cory had pledged to protect with her life.

Sealing their agreement with a grin and handshake made things tidy and complete. But it also created desolation within Cory. That emotion, Cory considered, left her with an unspoken tear inside her heart. The two women embarked on a love affair that rapidly shot across the many plateaus of romance. In record time, Cory fell deeply in love with the expat. Gabrielle laced daisies on the pillow beside her waking lover each morning they spent together. How could one not be captivated, Cory questioned.

And so, Gab's background, although sparsely accounted for, was only derived from snippets of conversation. French was fluently spoken by the expat. From this the information was derived that Gab's mother was from France and they'd often visited when Gab was a child.

From a discussion on Cory's father, who was a high ranking military man, came the fact that Gab's father had died a year ago. When Cory mentioned her own two siblings, Gab offered that she was an only child. Bits and pieces were what Cory had to accept. It was the best she would probably ever do.

Cory's rapid side-glance at her own reflection in the leaded window pane of the Lioness Tavern confirmed that she looked fine. She was to meet with Gab, and it was important that she feel confident. She'd worn heather-gray woolen trousers with a cotton tailored blouse. It was an outfit in which she felt comfortable traveling. She'd slung her large handbag over one shoulder. Hanging from one of the straps was a folded plaid jacket. Her other arm was loaded with a pyramid of books she needed to return to Gabrielle. A worn, pepper-colored umbrella dangled from its cord and was fastened to her wrist.

Although she took pride in wearing her captain's uniform, Cory also enjoyed shedding it and getting into less regimented civvies. Her final glimpse into the glass reassured her that her short, satiny waves of hair were in place. The glistening brunette curls framed a tawny peach complexion. Cory's skin was silky smooth, and her dimples were pronounced. A bright milky smile was her way of rewarding the kindness of others. Or her lover. Cobalt-hued eyes converted to the color of wisteria in different lighting conditions. Those eyes housed intelligence, warmth, and decency.

With a rapid patting down of her collar, she entered the lesbian pub. The door yawned closed behind her.

Mid-afternoon in the wedge-shaped Lioness Tavern was unusually quiet. Only a few of the regular patrons, punters, conversed in a low buzzing, and occasional spurts of laughter. Cory was appreciative of the relative quiet. That meant time alone with Gabrielle. She disliked the radical women who swarmed around her lover. They were mostly university women with similar persuasions. They circled around their table - and around Gab as if they were actually a pack of lioness sentries protecting their leader. Hence, Cory guessed, evolved the Lioness Tavern's sobriquet of the *den*.

Cory felt ill at ease when those women held court with Gab. Not only because they were all fiercely anti-American, but each member was also a part of the group they called their *Aesthetics Circle*. The elitist women were artists, dancers, actors, composers, musicians, writers, and poets. Cory was saluted in her own profession, but felt excluded, and certainly was made to feel inferior, by Gab's assemblage.

Gabrielle was primarily a poet. Published in literary magazines, her poetry, tightly-knit essays, and scathing articles reflected Gabrielle's wrath. Gab called herself a poetical diarist. But even that description failed to explain her.

Cory would never fit in with Gab's friends, and she questioned how she could have fallen so deeply in love with someone so opposite. She was never the *groupie* type of woman. She was a strong leader, a decisive person of authority. She read primarily non-fiction. Gab offered only the controversy of invention. Artistically, politically, the women were polarized in opposite directions. But each time they met, Cory admitted, there was a depth of unexplainable love.

She had anticipated each leave. She would voyage across the channel, and rush to Gab's side. It was undeniable, for love always brought her back to London.

But this was to be her last visit to London during this tour of duty. She would be traveling away from Gab on a transport. Later that evening she was returning to Germany. From there she would be flown stateside for a brief visit with her family. Then her deployment would be to a dangerous war zone.

She scanned the den. Cory felt a jab of sorrow. She'd already begun the dread of a good-bye. Memories of Gab in the Lioness Den would be recalled with longing. She studied the nuances. Caricatures, portraits and photos of lesbian legends were hung along the mahogany-paneled walls. Sappho, Cather, Stein, and Hall were women of yesteryear. Added were photos of Etheridge, Lang, Navratilova, Tomlin, and DeGeneres. Many other lesbians were recognized, and a few not.

The Lioness was done in late Victorian décor. It offered a stalwart ambience. With carved woodwork, gleaming beams, ornate plaster ceilings, polished brassware, and stained-glass windows, the room was of another century. Warmth exuded, but it was with the historic look of being shopworn.

Cory spotted Gabrielle resting on a banquette seat against the back wall. Gab glanced up from the book she was perusing. She quickly stood, beckoning Cory to her side. "I wasn't expecting you so early," Gab's resonant voice exclaimed as she clasped her lover in her warm embrace. "I thought you'd be in later tonight." There was a soothing cadence in her speech. As if she were reading a poem, she whispered, "I'm glad you're early. More time."

"Not really. My orders arrived this morning. I'll need to catch a flight back later this evening. I'm scheduled on a transport back home in the morning. I left early to spend as much time together as we can. I'm sorry." Words caught in Cory's throat. "I tried to call." Her voice halted with a pronounced sting. "I'm sorry. It's all so rushed. I had no control."

"Military dictators," Gab said with subdued anger.

"Gab, I can't change the orders."

"So we won't even have a final night together?"

"No. I tried to delay. It wasn't possible." Cory pressed her shoulders back against the bench's seat as she and her lover settled. She leaned her umbrella in the corner. Then she placed the books and handbag on the table in front of Gab.

It seemed natural, even uneventful, that Gabrielle automatically ordered her lover a pint of ale. There was disappointment in her eyes when she placed the frothy drink in front of Cory. She lifted her own mug. "So this is a final toast."

"Gab, I'm sorry." Displayed were her burning eyes that blinked back tears. "We have a few hours before I need to return. I wish it were different."

"Your monster commands. Going into this we knew that one day our *farewell* would catch up with us."

Cory sipped her drink. For the first time she tasted bitterness. Her own, as well as the ale. "Gab, I don't want to leave you. I'm going to miss you."

"I'll miss you, too." Gabrielle's glance lowered. "For me it's just another parting. Another fortuitous, flipping farewell. Another of life's incomplete episodes. I've lived them before." She attempted a robot's expression. "But this time I'm truly being torn apart." She tousled her hair. "You know that I'm in love with you," her discordant voice admitted.

"Remember when we met and both agreed that nothing is

forever. We both promised that our parting would be okay. Well, it isn't okay at all." Cory wondered if the silence meant Gab was thinking about their meeting months ago. She dammed back her own tears. It seemed like yesterday when they first traded smiles. Had Cory worn her uniform while visiting Trafalgar Square that day, Gabrielle wouldn't have even glanced in her direction. Or perhaps she might have issued a scowl at the attractive officer.

Once Gabrielle became aware of Cory's military career, the battle lines were drawn. Their ceasefire allowed the lovers a slim chance. With trips to England's parks, cathedrals, and galleries, love seemed to be a rescue mission for each woman. They shared picnics in the country sides, seaside excursions, and romance that became as automatic an event as either woman had ever experience. Their love was weaved on the Queen's Roads, but it became a precarious journey for their hearts. Separation was inevitable.

Every spare moment of every leave Cory spent rendezvousing with her lover. From neatly packed hampers of food in the Dales, to fish and chips in SoHo, the women seemed to be one. Two hearts invested in one another. Now, Cory sensed a detachment. She wondered how calm Gabrielle really was.

Cory was obviously not relaxed, nor did she pretend to be. She couldn't refrain from thinking about their wondrous lovemaking. It had been the first time she'd experienced the depths of orgasmic pleasure. She had finally allowed her barriers to drop. Emotions triumphed as never before. Gabrielle had been the only woman she'd allowed free reign. During her thirty-five years, Cory had hidden so many of her feelings. But Gab was allowed to enter previously locked emotions. Gabrielle also admitted that the syncopation of their braided bodies was unique to her.

They mutually explored one another's nakedness. But their minds remained sequestered from the probe. Their initial vow made certain of that. Now, Cory wanted access to her lover's thoughts - the ones that reached so deeply they nearly buried themselves. She wanted more.

Without hesitation, she blurted, "Gab, we have so little time left. Please allow me to know you. *You.*"

A faint grin appeared on Gab's face. "Having shared everything two women's bodies can share, I'd say we know one another. We've certainly memorized one another."

"We've exchanged our flesh. Not our minds."

"Cory, you've read my work. Those are my thoughts. Me. And

I've heard all of your propaganda I care to hear."

"Our parting is hurting me more than you."

"Captain Daniels, *you're* the one doing the leaving. I'm where I was when we met. And I'm sorrier than you'll ever know that I'm losing you. But make no mistake, you're furloughing me. You're being shipped out. You are ending the relationship. I'll be right here."

"So where do we go from here? I have no choice. Has it crossed your mind that you don't have any binds to London? When I am released...." she paused, hoping that she'd live to her early retirement. "We can make plans. In a few years my twenty years will be complete. You can return to the U.S. with me."

"Return?" Gabrielle grimaced. "Cory, don't *you* understand. I'm in pain. I would love to have plans with you. Returning isn't an option."

"If you really love me...."

"Cory, don't do that to me. Part of our pact was that we valiantly attempt not to hurt one another."

"We don't need to be hurt."

"If I follow you – I'll be hurt. No, Cory. Our love is a great universal romance. I've been preparing for my sadness. You'll leave. I'll stay."

"You view our love as some romantic interlude? A script of parting?" Her eyes closed. She felt the wrenching of her stomach. Her heart constricted before beating wildly with anger. "I'm in love with you."

"So how much loss do you want to see in my face?" Gabrielle's eyes were moist. Her words twisted through her lips. "Our love has been a complete minefield. So now the soldier goes away. I'm the one left with memories on every street corner. Every time we visited a place, it became *ours*. I'm the one who will feel the emotional detonation of a bomb ripping my heart to shreds each time I walk a footpath we've shared."

"We can make plans to be together again." Cory required a plan. She needed someone to be there for her. She needed Gabrielle to be there. To be waiting.

"I can't. I won't return to the U.S. If you're waiting for me to pledge undying love, to tell you I'll follow you into hell, save it. I'm not one of your obedient troops. I'm not in your branch of the military. I don't take orders, Captain."

Through her teeth she replied, "I do take orders. It's my

profession. Gab, if it were possible, I'd stay with you. It isn't."

"But I'm supposed to follow your lead. Or maybe you'd like me to pitch my lovelorn body from the Dover Cliffs." She briefly reminisced their day at Dover Castle. That was the first exchange of the word *love*.

"Dover Castle. I remember you gave me the key to your pension and a tiny key that you said was the key to your heart. But it must not have been." Cory carried that key in a locket around her neck. She'd wanted to believe it was all possible.

"Now you want me in the brig. Or maybe you'd like me to do a stint in the Tower or a detachment to the guillotine?"

"I don't want your sadness, Gab."

Gabrielle's hands covered her eyes a moment. "Cory, you're officious tone isn't going to ease my solitude."

Cory issued a wintry glare. "We *can* be together again."

"Not likely. No." She breathed in deeply, completely. "Damn. I should have the art of losing people down to a science. But listen carefully, I'll never leave London. This is now my home. You *knew* that when we met."

"We weren't in love when we met." Her voice quivered. Her eyes were tormented. "I'm not leaving because it's my choice."

"You're leaving because of duty to your country. And you want my sacrifice in going back to that same country. I've already sacrificed. Your government has seen to that."

"Tell me about your sacrifice, Gab. Since you brought it up, I'd like to know." Cory turned her mug of ale. She endured a static silence. "Please. I truly want to know. I'm breaking apart because I no longer have the words to combat your emotionally self-contained prison." She reached to give Gabrielle's handcuff a turn. "So tell me about your sacrifice?"

"It's nothing to do with you."

"Please. Tell me?" Tears bundled in her eyes.

"Where's that military ramrod stiff upper lip? I'm supposed to be the fragile artist. We have a role reversal here." Gab's words fluttered, but there was a stir of irritation.

"Are you trying to be glib? Can't we turn off your cynical dry wit for a few hours? Our few remaining hours?" Cory inhaled. The scent of ale and smoke overpowered her lover's usual minty fragrance. "I'll miss everything about you, Gab. I'll miss you more than I've ever missed anyone or anything in my life."

"But you've got your orders." There was a hermetically sealed finality to Gabrielle's voice. "Let's face facts. I'm not the one with two silver bars on my uniform. I'm not fighting for God and Country. I'm not the missile-totting mama. You can take off your uniform and put down your weapons. You can stay."

"You know I can't. Won't."

"This is my home now."

"It isn't your *home!*" Cory spat. Her eyes narrowed. "You're an American citizen. This is England."

"Citizenship is tricky. I'm an expatriate." Gabrielle's arms crossed. Her stare was riveted to Cory's. Both women wished to extrapolate a message. "I'm the same person in the same place where you first met me. Stop acting like I'm the one vacating our love."

"What about your family in America. You must have ties?"

"We agreed to respect one another's privacy." She seemed to bite off the end of the sentence. Her word-stash of anger ended. "Please, Cory."

"The Brits would call you bloody-minded."

Amused, Gab chided, "The Yanks would call me worse."

"I'd hoped love might make you feel differently."

"You've been well-indoctrinated. You live within the constraints of hypocrisy. You've been propagandized with illusive meanings."

"At least you know the reasons I love my country. I have no idea why you're on this obsessive crusade against our country."

"Our? Got a mouse in your pocket?" Gab teased. "Or is that the jargon the military uses to unify?" Gabrielle stood, fished her pockets for coins, and then threw them on the table. She extended her hand. "Let's go back to my place. I've got some excellent Yorkshire bitter. I purchased some great bread, cheeses, and even champagne grapes. And I want to hold you."

Through steamy rains, the women walked. Gabrielle stopped in front of a misted storefront window. With her index finger, she drew their initials. Around them she drew a heart. She took Cory's hand. The wetness of Gabrielle's fingers excited Cory.

While ambling to Gab's dreary room, there was quietude. As if each spirit needed time to consider their own litany of regret, they walked. When Cory saw the small pension, she felt her throat constrict. She'd often considered that it was their love nest within the rancid gullet of a hidden ghetto. It was theirs. Today the room would be a friend she would be bidding farewell.

Known as *poofter palace* because of the many gay men residing in the tattered old structure, it had housed many of Cory's most lovely memories. Usually there were tenants coming and going. Today it was still. Even the swath of roses near the fence had faded since her last visit. The pension was where she'd placed her heart. She knew that this time she must take her heart along with her when she left.

She wouldn't be returning. With resolute stoicism, she stepped through the entryway.

* * *

Gabrielle's arms winged outward as the women propped against a hill of pillows. "Let's make our final hours sweet," she suggested. With a smile that was barely there, she reached to touch Cory's shoulder. Her mouth followed the caress, trailing up the neck of her lover. "Cory, we can make these hours the sweetest parting two lovers have ever known," she whispered.

Cory felt forlorn. She knew Gab's words were true, for there had never been another love that had been so deep. "Passion. Yes, complete ecstasy. But Gab, this may be our final time we're ever together. And I don't know the woman I've fallen in love with. Would it be possible to share the total contents of our hearts?" Cory sat, pulling from Gab's embrace. "Please?"

"Why now?"

"Gab, we're parting." Cory's stare locked with Gabrielle's. "You know me well enough to know that I hate breaking a vow. But I'd like one parting gift from you. I want to break our pledge."

"I get it. Permission to forget our promise."

"I want to know why you arbor hatred for our country. I need to know."

"Curiosity? You want secrets revealed *now*?" Gab's eyes were penetrating. Her back became an iron spine. "Now?"

"Don't look at me like that."

"Until now we've stayed out of the quicksand."

"I want to understand the granite slabs you have around your secret."

"I'm not enigmatic to hurt others. Only to protect me. My mystery is mine. Let it be." Gabrielle kicked off her loafers. She unbuttoned her blouse, exposing her smallish breasts. Her eyes flickered. "Damn, I'm not trying to break into your history."

"I've told you my secrets. You know everything about me. I'm not hiding my past from you."

"I'm not a pistol-packing patriot, so I must be a villain. That's the only answer you truly want. We're two different people with different perspectives. How we got here isn't that important. I accept that you're an American warrior."

"I serve my country to maintain your freedom. Your freedom of speech is one of those freedoms I protect with the military you hate. That freedom gives you the right to spew your anger at our country. I've pledged to uphold, and to die for, your right to dissent. For our freedom."

"Freedom!" Gabrielle leaned back. "Your indoctrination is complete. And who the hell appointed the United States to be the universe's social conscience? Let's just stop there. We can't win."

"No. Because you won't tell my why you feel the way you do. It's ironic that you make your living from American dollars."

"I provide words and those words are paid for by various financial enterprises. That's the economy of it. Unlike your paycheck, mine has nothing to do with your government. My fight isn't with the people. It's the politics that are unconscionable."

"People elect my government."

"Usually only slightly over half vote a candidate in. And many citizens are somnambulists. They mark the box of the politician spending the most funds. They buy into all that talk of civil liberty."

"So you ran out on our country because it isn't perfect? You don't agree with all the objectives. But what are your convictions about? And if truth and justice mean so much, why don't you stand your ground and fight for America?"

Gabrielle's lips closed completely - resolutely. She inspected the blank wall. Banality hung. The hush continued for many moments before she spoke. "I've severed my prior ties. I was many people in my past. One of them was patriotic." Her eyelids lowered, clamping tightly. "I'm no longer that person."

"I don't believe that person has moved on. Gab, that person is still sending out signals. I believe your hurt has converted into hatred. I want to know why you've changed."

"We all change."

"Will you stop being evasive! I'm asking why you've turned tail and why you ran." Cory recognized a glint of anger in Gabrielle's eyes. She had found her lover's hot button. She pushed onward. "I've always been taught that running is cowardly." If she were ever to know the truth, it might assist in changing Gab's mind. But the price for extracting the truth might be hurting Gab. If it allowed resolution, Cory weighed, it might be worth the cost. It might be their only chance for a future together. "Well, where was your courage?"

"Your military rhetoric is crap." Gabrielle's words were thrusts. "I left an intolerant land devoid of flavor and texture. Bigotry is glossed over. Your sexual orientation is concealed from your precious military. Don't ask and don't tell. That's a noble way to play hide and seek. Courage in a closet? You're a woman. You're a lesbian. The government is run by a majority of straight males. Those ethical exemplars promise not to search you out, but don't let them catch you being out. Some flipping deal."

"So you run to England to crybaby. Expat! What the hell is that, Gab? You're a malcontent."

"I'd leave that arrow in its quiver, Captain. You don't have a clue," Gabrielle seethed. She quickly buttoned her blouse, fumbling with each buttonhole. Lurching from the bed, she poured a glass of beer. After a hasty, harsh gulp, she whirled back to face Cory. "You just don't know."

"What I know is that I've spent the most wonderful, fun months of my life at your side. I want to know why we can't continue. Explain it to me."

"The United States of America's original intent has been bastardized. It's no longer the land our parents and grandparents fought to create. And save. My father...." Her face blanched chalk white. "The system of justice has been turned over by federal thugs. And the youth of American knows it. They're overwhelmed. Look at them. Drugged up, drowned in excess. They've lost their way. *Your* country is on the decline. The system has been violated. And you're one of the guards. You're protecting power and capital gain. And now they're sending young people off to a sand pile for oil. Profits for the politicians."

"I'm fighting to make the world better. We might be able to make it better for the women of that sand pile? How about giving foreign people a chance at justice?"

"America needs to start sweeping its own doorstep," Gabrielle insisted.

"Then after my tour of duty, why don't you return with me. Let's begin fighting for our beliefs. I'll join you in trying to make it better."

"Restoration is a little late. The government needs to be purged."

"The rehabilitation of freedom is cumbersome. It may be flawed." Cory's face flushed. "But that's not a reason to leave. You put that handcuff on and go moaning across an ocean. Did America's injustice chase you away, or do you enjoy your role of being a self-imposed exile?"

"Haven't you got a plane to catch?"

"My country isn't perfect, but it's the best I've seen."

"Most lost civilizations maintain that attitude. My county, right or wrong. Why am I even wasting my time? You just couldn't allow my beliefs to go unchallenged."

"I may not respect your beliefs, but it doesn't mean I don't respect you."

"That leaves us with two options. We either make love, or I call you a cab."

Tears forged in the corners of Cory's eyes. "Hate is like an impact crater. You have the scars. But I don't know what impacted you. Call it a going away gift. Tell me what has hurt you. Let me understand why the greatest love of my life is being sacrificed."

"You're walking way. You're going onto a dangerous battleground where *you're* willing to sacrifice your life. That would also be my sacrifice since I'm in love with you. And it would be for nothing but the lying, greedy, money grubbing politicians. And they don't give a damn about anyone or anything other than profit."

"I'm serving my country. I'm not thrilled with the idea of spending my future getting shot at. Gab, I do love you. If you love me as you say, tell me why you're so angry." Cory's gaze was a direct hit. "My love deserves that much."

"Love doesn't need explanations or excuses."

"Please."

Gabrielle sat at the small wooden dinette table. She poured beer slowly, deliberately. When Cory sat opposite her, she filled her lover's glass. "I'll explain. Then I want you to leave."

"If that's what you want."

"You might think I'm some treasonous bitch for the sake of being angry. Well, I am damned angry. When you leave, it's as though another dream is being stolen from me. My story begins with an ultimate belief in the American dream. A middle-aged man has worked diligently for many years. He meets and marries a young French woman. She is artistic, sensitive, and loving. They adore one another. The woman helps her husband build their small newspaper into their empire - a chain of suburban newspapers. By the time their only child is grown, they are wealthy beyond their dreams."

"But that's a wonderful story."

"It would have been. They hired a disreputable accountant. He made a pass at the man's beautiful wife. She rejected him, told the husband, and the accountant was fired. But the accountant had tinkered with the books. He'd skimmed profits, and then went on to incriminate the couple. Tax fraud. Coiled like a snake, after the rebuff and firing, he went to the IRS with bogus files. Render to the government. Not anticipating any problems, because my parents were innocent, and believed in the courts, they were unprepared.""What kind of monster was this accountant? Aren't there remedies?""The accountant had gambling debts, and the government was promising him a percentage of their take. The couple had always been exemplar citizens. Charitable, kind, honest, good people. The accountant had an ugly background. It didn't matter. The government was going to make an example of the couple. Both the treasury and the accountant were going to reap the monetary rewards. The accountant had set my parents up with such a precision fraud, it was an ironclad case. My parents were indicted." Streamers of thought silenced her.

Cory's hand reached to grasp Gabrielle's limp fingers. "What happened to them?"

"My father worked out a plea bargain so that my mother wouldn't face charges. Their fortune was lost. My father went to Federal prison. My mother completely broke down. She's now in a sanitarium. After serving several months, my father was released."

"The government finally got it right?"

"No. It was evidence dug up by reporters. The accountant's gambling debts were revealed, the entire fraud was unearthed. He was pressured into confessing. The press was relentless in their efforts to vindicate my father. They not only exposed the accountant, but also over-zealous IRS agents. My father was completely exonerated. Between court costs, legal fees, and my mother's medical bills, there was nothing left of their American dream. The government sent regrets. Records were expunged."

"And now?"

"My mother remains institutionalized. My father visited her every day until he died last year. My mother doesn't recognize anyone. She'll never know the bad dream is over. Nor does she know her beloved husband has died. Death from a broken heart. Maybe she's lucky to be in her own safe zone."

Tears slid over Gabrielle's cheeks. It was the only complete emotion Cory had seen Gab express. "I'm so sorry. Gab, come back with me. After my tour we can help care for your mother. We can work it out together. I've fallen in love with you."

"If that's true, stay with me."

"You know I can't." She squeezed her lover's hand. "It will only be another six months. I'll request another tour of Europe."

"I can't leave London."

"Gab, we can be together. We can change things. We'll dedicate our lives to it."

"We're on opposite sides. We can never be together as long as your career military."

"I'm not the enemy."

"Cory, you vowed never to extract my anthem from me. You broke that vow. Now you want me to give up my beliefs. I just can't. And I'm not strong enough to lose you in a war that I'll never believe in."

"If I have you, I promise I'll come back," Cory promised.

"I love you too much to take another chance. I've lost the people I love."

"It's my duty. I've got to go."

"I won't ever again need to anguish over someone I love when they're taken from me.

I'll always love you." Gabrielle threw her jacket over her shoulder. She walked to the door. "I'm going for a walk. Lock up when you leave."

Cory rushed to the door. She felt the breeze from its closing. There was stiffness from her sob as it plumed through her heart and then her lips. She recognized how much she loved Gabrielle. The extent of her feelings couldn't overturn her loyalty to her country. She believed that Gab would not turn around and come back into her arms. Gabrielle's reason for hatred was justified.

Gabrielle had declared her anthem. It was simple. Love required too much.

Cory gathered her belongings. She locked the door behind her. She slid the key through the letter chute.

She wished she would have made love with Gabrielle. At least she would have had a lovely parting memory to take away with her. The sky's low ceiling of pearl gray clouds bit into her flesh with afternoon's coolness.

Passing by the initialed window pane, Cory paused. Steam had nearly obliterated the letters inside the faintly drawn heart. Cory pressed her face against the misty window. She sobbed into the heartbeat that was coming from the glass.

She didn't understand why time that had been designated for love had been used for anything except romance. For the first time in her life, Cory didn't want to go home. She didn't want to attempt to sort out *where her home* might be. She cursed her feelings.

She cursed boundaries. She considered that one day when the world settles into sanity and the wars ends, hatred and greed might dissipate. Perhaps, everyone would be home.

The delicate boundaries of war could be alleviated. But what if there was a strike against the United States of America by foreign terrorists? What if there was one terrible moment of being intruded upon? Cory paused. What if it became too painful without Gab?

Pellet-sized raindrops drummed her face when she looked up to curse the heavens. Her uncertainty made her ache to run after Gab. They could become the world's vagabonds. They could love as surely as the memories of laughter and joy. Reality was far different than the pain of being homesick. Home, her tribal belonging, her military family, was hidden. As hidden as she must be. And there was no next question.

She only knew she had a transport waiting to take her somewhere.

Cory heard the sound of someone scurrying around the corner.

"You can't leave like this." Gabrielle sob stuck in her throat. "I need you, Cory."

As Cory turned, she collapsed against Gab. "We will need to fight a war together, without your hatred. No matter how justified it might be."

Gab lifted her hand. She pulled up her shirt sleeve. "My cuff. You have the key in your locket. But if you release me, I've got to know we'll always be there for one another. That you'll understand my personal war."

Cory opened her locket, and then twisted the key to release Gab's cuff. When it clattered to the ground, she spoke solemnly. "When I retire, we'll go back to *our* country. Together we'll make every effort to change the system. We can do it."

"I'll wait for you. We'll be together as much as we can. Whenever we can be together." Their embrace was strong.

Cory frowned. "Gab, with all the differences and beliefs we have, I'm not sure we can make it."

"I'm not sure we *can't*." A smile appeared. It was bright and unrehearsed. It was the truest smile, Cory had seen. "In fact I think we *can* make it together. One thing I know. We've got to make the attempt. For now, let's go back to the apartment. Let's hold one another. We have a few hours before you need to leave. We can make plans."

Cory grinned. "Yes. I'll even memorize your poetry."

"Captain, I'll *sanitize* it for you." Cory sweetly kissed her lover. "I'll always be waiting for you to return."

"I promise I'll make every effort to return to you."

As they hand in hand walked the cracked sidewalk, they both felt an optimism that had been missing in their relationship. Approaching the entryway of the pension, they heard the loud, erratic sounding radio. From inside, a voice blared news of planes hitting towers. The announcement was chilling. New York. The Twin Towers.

The Captain and the Expat would be facing their greatest challenges together. Cory thought of the heart Gabrielle had drawn. Both of their initials were inside the heart.

Inside the heart was where they belonged.

Photograph by Kathie Solie

FRIVOLITY AMONGST FRIENDS

Mid-1980s Meeting

They'd met a quarter of a century ago, in the early 1960s. That was when blondes had their own dynasty of jokes. The three blondes became roommates. Tenuous were the sixties. Living became invigorated as it transitioned past the humdrum fifties. It began on a Nebraska campus. The women met, became roommates, friends, and confidants.

Each reunion was a step backward. The women's twenty-fifth college homecoming had been held months ago. And it had been so enjoyed that the trio agreed to meet later in the year for their own private reunion. Each of the three agreed that they hadn't truly had enough time together during the two-day event in Nebraska.

It was in the bustling mid-eighties. Technology, finance, and peace, were the order of the day. Times had changed; the women had perhaps changed even more.

Dr. Jane Cassidy's yearbook photo portrayed a young women set on success. She had gone on to finish college, medical school, internship, residency, and she founded a flourishing medical practice. Gynecology was, so to speak, a wide open field for women MDs. Not only did she appreciate women's company better than men's, she appreciated women far better than men.

However, she disputed, she had not selected her profession as much as she had been chosen by it. It was highly suggested by professors. Female medical doctors caring for other women seemed to be the modern trend. And Jane loved thinking of herself as a trendsetter. Although her lesbian friends teased her about not getting enough of a good thing, she declined comment. She'd heard it all before.

Her yearbook photo also reflected a serious frown. Her periwinkle-blue eyes lit with humor, but also narrowed with earnest concern. Her eyes had not changed. Now, patting down her taupe and gray mixed hair, her fingers systematically rolled back to fidget with the bun at the base of her neck. She thought her hairdo to be distinguished. *Esteemed* was a look she was going for even back in those university days. Her face was fleshier, her lips less coral, and they lifted up into a smile less often. Time had pressed a few small bunches of wrinkles around her creamy complexion. She'd added a few pounds around her midsection, although daily exercise had kept her shapely and fairly well-toned. All in all, she felt satisfied about her plight in life. Achievements were hers.

Nanette Rogers had taken a far different path. She'd joined academia. Marrying a fellow professor in haste had proved a mistake. Her divorce took longer than the marriage lasted. She persisted. She selected a less cerebral man next. But that had only lasted five repugnant years. She complained that he was like a coyote poised at a rabbit's hole every night of the year. She did not reside in the throes of passion where he concerned.

Although men liked her strawberry-blonde hair, her huge topaz eyes, and apricot lips, she decided twice-bitten – she would also be shy in duplicate. Her smile remained warm and bright, her dialogue terse and witty. The professor had no intention of resuming matrimony's dice toss. She continued to decline offers to set her up on blind dates. She wasn't certain where life's path had aimed itself, but she was optimistic that she was bright enough to never again stampede the aisle of matrimony.

Celeste Prichard had big goals - had bigger knockers. Somehow, her enormous promise overshadowed even those attributes. She'd leaned her shapely body, with those well-endowed bosoms, against an older billionaire boss. Godfrey Murray had made his billions throughout the sixties by providing espionage equipment during the Viet Nam War. After the war, he turned his attention to commercial surveillance equipment. Celeste had quickly become aware of his celebrated wealth, and gave a wiggle.

She was relocated to a penthouse while her boss detached from his first wife. Then, with a blink of her olive-green eyes, took vows to forever comfort her man. In early days, her rosy face was painted by make-up experts. Later, when wrinkles originated, she met a Palm Beach surgeon. He not only took care of her face – but also her orgasms, and her sense of excitement. Celeste's platinum hair took Florida's Gold Coast by storm. A multitude of males, including a tennis coach, swarmed.

Her husband, Celeste confided to friends, never suspected. She gave him three wonderful male heirs, to go with his two female heirs from the first marriage. She was given two luxury homes, jazzy autos, and social connections. He'd been given whatever he wanted. He wasn't the type to deny his foxy wife anything. She explained, he had also probably had a fling or two along the matrimonial highway. She insisted on final approval of his private secretaries. However, she wasn't terribly concerned. There was no pre-nuptial hindering her best interest. She was a steel ribbon. And a crafty one at that.

The blonde trio had promised to meet again at The Breakers in Palm Beach. They would do it up right. Because Celeste lived in Palm, she was there to make the arrangements. Their suites were definitely magnificent and adjoining.

They each anticipated the meeting that was certain to provide total enjoyment with ritualistic flair. Jane and Nanette had met many times over the years. After Jane's graduation from medical school she had resided in San Diego. But she had conferenced in New York, where Professor Nanette Rogers had home based. Neither woman had seen much of Celeste after she'd relocated to Palm Beach.

Nebraska had seemed light years away from their youth. Celeste often joked that she had gone to Nebraska because no other university would have her. And she was reminded that her major skill was as society editor of her campus newspaper. Her senior year, she had broken *every* iota of gossip. After graduation, she became editor of the college alumni newsletter. Inference and innuendo often made it into those yellow sheets. She vowed to keep her editorship until death.

Jane and Nanette met in the lobby, checked in, and got ready for dinner. They met back at the restaurant. Nanette complained, "I knew Celeste was going to be late. She lives in the city, and we travel from across the country. But she's going to be fashionably late."

"Nan, I told her six PM sharp. She'll be here at five after six."

"But it's five-thirty now."

"Exactly. That gives us half an hour to chat without her."

"Brilliant, doc," Nanette grinned as she followed her former roommate into the dining room. They were led to their table. "Gives us time for a quick bracer."

Smirking, Jane commented, "We're finally on Celeste's timetable." After they were seated, she sighed deeply. "I really wanted to have a few minutes to talk with you alone before she arrives. I confess, it is contemptible of me but at times I really wonder how we managed to room with her."

After ordering cocktails, Nanette agreed, "I was actually glad that our reunion kept us busy. Especially that Celeste was kept busy. But she put these plans together so quickly, I didn't know how to get out of it. I did want to see you again though."

"So back in school, you also had thoughts of tossing her out of our three-story dorm?"

"A constant longing." Nanette lifted her scotch and soda to toast, "Here's to us. Hell, back then we planned all this. We figured we'd be dilapidated old broads, ready to fall into an open grave. But I feel young and alive."

Jane's husky voice concurred, "Yes. We were so young. We were years away from being old. It seemed like centuries back then. However, I don't feel old either."

"You don't look old."

Their eyes linked. Jane was certain that Nanette suspected her sexual orientation. But she had never mentioned it. Celeste, on the other hand, had no earthly idea, and would certainly be jolted if she knew.

Jane's forehead gathered into a frown. "Remember when Celeste told us we were both far too intelligent to ever be happy."

Nanette laughed. "I'd forgotten about that. Yes, I recall she claimed we weren't ethereal enough to become good wives. She pities us. She has Godfrey. She sends that poor old sucker out to work. He's had two coronaries."

"And multiple cases of executive tight sphincter syndrome."

Nanette snickered. "Celeste believes her rightful place is in the shopping malls. Sorry if I'm being tacky, but she is such a tart."

"She asked *what* half a dozen times when I explained that biology doesn't predestine a woman's roll. She'd asked how a woman could be a doctor. But then she believes the society pages are what rotate the world. She's such a *wife*."

Nanette shook her head in agreement. "Once she stated that we had her sympathy. One of us hadn't snagged a man; the other couldn't keep one. When I said that we have our freedom, she said we must be very envious of her."

"I'm happier alone. Unless the right person happens into my life."

"I certainly don't know how to select husbands, so I guess I'm better off with my books. I always do just fine in the library."

"Nan, what really happened to your marriages?"

Shrugging, Nanette issued a quick poignant grin. "My first

husband was of the old school. My second hadn't even attended school. What can I say?"

"It wasn't the sex?"

"To be honest, I have confusion. According to my *good girl* upbringing sex wasn't supposed to be fun. And wasn't."

Jane's eyebrows lifted. "As I recall you were always frightened of burning in hell's most vicious incinerator. Once you told me you'd end up a charcoal crisp for petting."

Nanette's raspy laugh caught up with Jane's chuckle. "I'd listened to all the myths. Then I went on to perpetuate them."

With a cynical looping of her thoughts, Jane considered that was one of the reasons she'd been reluctant to share her experiences with Nanette. She respected her roommate enough not to want to foul her religious nest. "The blazing passion was quite the topic in our dorm. Going *all the way* was a stain on the reputation. Not that it wasn't going on – it was like sex in a rabbit hutch. It wasn't bragged about like now."

"All the way. Yes, I remember that old expression. Now the students just ask one another if the sex was out of this world. Liberation, huh? The guys are still scoring, but the women are also moaning if they haven't gotten any. They credit the pill with having created all that talk of sexual freedom. The Mod generation also had a big impact."

"Liberation or not, women still have questions."

"And they ask you?"

"Yes. Some do. But some are still inhibited about talking with their gynecologist."

"Doctor Jane," Nanette began mockingly, but then her tone withered. "Think maybe there might be something wrong with me?"

"Your marriages didn't satisfy you?"

"Not in that way. No."

Inhaling deeply, Jane peered through the eyewear she'd just put on to check the wine's list. "Well, Nan, I've always thought of you as a sexually robust woman. Or at I suspected you have the potential to be very amorous."

"The inclination is there. I just never feel *mentally sensual*."

"I understand." Jane lowered her head. She'd wanted to take Nanette on a trip to Lesbos so many times. She'd wanted to kiss her, but never dared. She watched as Nanette crossed her long legs. She hoped Nan wasn't reading her mind, or her desires. "Do you want to tell me about it?"

"Jane, sex has always been a sort of voodoo science of one's genitalia. It just never seemed to happen for me."

Their glance latched. Jane's hunger was as hidden as she could make it. Even after all these years, she admitted, she wanted Nanette. And perhaps she always had. When her relationships broke apart, her first thought was Nanette. Always. Now she wanted to probe the disclosure of discontented sex, but as always, the timing was amiss.

She looked up to see Celeste Prichard Murray making her entrance. Celeste waved as she made her way to the table. With bust nearly exposed in a low-cut sundress, She exploded onto the scene.

Nanette leaned near Jane. "I swear her huge boobs make her look as though she should be the prow head on a pirate vessel."

"Oh, you two," Celeste hooted as the women stood to give quick embraces. "Look at how wonderful you two are keeping." When their branching hug ended, the women sat. Celeste squashed her hourglass body down with vigor. She squealed, "We're together again - the blonde trio!"

There was a communion of sorts. There was also, Jane sensed, an isolation.

Perhaps that isolation had always been. Time intensified it. "You're looking happy, well, and wealthy."

"And you're the doctor," Celeste whooped, "so I must be in great shape. I really figured you'd quit medical school when I sent you that clipping about the glut of doctors. But you're obviously making a living. Naturally, I hoped you'd find a good man before you got too many years on the odometer. You're attractive in a funny sort of way."

Amused, Jane stammered, "Thank you, I guess."

"Well, you do know that too much mileage on the old clock makes men dash off. You know," Celeste babbled, "when you finished school, I thought to myself, well that's her MD. Now, can her MRS be far behind. It has been," she emphasized with a giggle. "Unless you have an announcement, I guess I can save my wedding gift monies."

"Celeste," Jane spoke dryly, "you never change."

"Thanks. They do wonders at the clinic." Celeste turned her attention to Nanette "And darling girl, I am absolutely *devastated* that your second divorce seemed to have kept you away from the altar all these years. I feel so badly for you."

"I'm truly fine."

Celeste leaned against the table. She quizzed, "Tell me, Nan, did your second husband's balls go funny?"

"What?" Nanette roared with laughter.

"I heard he had something or other."

"What he had aside from stupidity, was a case of other women," Nanette confessed with a smile so faintly draw that it was almost oblivious.

"Well, I don't recall my source. I'd just heard the juicy tidbit that he had a disease. Of course, I disclaimed it as ruthless gossip."

"Glad you didn't put it in the alumni news," Nanette joked. "Before I had the chance to disclaim it. Those kinds of disclaimers are always buried in small letters beneath an advertisement for penis enhancers or some damned thing."

"That alumni news!" Celeste said with bubbling fury, "It will be the death of me. I work so hard gathering news. I can't even find half the alumni."

"Not to worry," Jane remarked, "I'm sure they can't escape you forever."

Celeste laughed, and then as if the gates of her giggles closed, she stopped. "I don't need to tell you two that I get to the bottom of every good story. If I hadn't married money, I'd have made a great gossip columnist. Some of those royal watchers really rake in the bucks. I always tell Godfrey that I'd have ended up with bundles of bucks regardless."

"I rather hope that my past marriages are off-limits as far as the press goes."

"Nanette, I'd never divulge a word. Sometimes men just go off of women. And what does that leaved a woman with? Nothing," Celeste answered her own question with rhetorical skill.

"Women can survive without men," Jane argued.

"I'd have expected you to say that, Jane darling. But look at poor, dear Nanette. She's looking rather drab without a man. You were always pale, but Nan did blossom when she was married."

"Her blood pressure was probably elevated," Jane offered. "But what you're implying is that a man should be my life."

"Jane Cassidy," Celeste's eyes batted as she spoke, "You're just being argumentative. Well, I'm not providing you with a verbal punching bag, as in the old days. I'm sure that in your case, well, to be rather indelicate, you take care of yourself in the sexual needs department."

"Meaning I am reduced to the fine art of masturbation?" Jane
bristled. The edge to her voice clearly reflected her displeasure.

"Honestly," Celeste blustered, "there are modern appliances. The
1980's technology has provided an absolute treasure trove of
gadgetry. You ought to see the surveillance devices Godfrey's
company produces. I mean, he doesn't have anything to do with such
things as vibrators. But it's all out there."

"You haven't answered my question. You assume I'm reduced to
a world of battery-operated imitations of male members."

"Jane, you're just trying to upset me. Let's talk about something
else now."

Nanette was aware of Celeste's 'accuse and run' game. "Yes,
let's talk about something else. Has Godfrey's balls gone funny?"

"Oh, you," Celeste's voice went childish. "I only wanted to
know why Jane never married."

"She must have been frightened you wouldn't approve," Nanette
sputtered. "Celeste, Jane is busy with a successful medical practice."

Jane deliberated a moment. With a tormented glance through the
maze of people gathering for dinner, she considered a response that
would shut Celeste up. "There have been lovers. Just no one special."

"How delicious!" Celeste quickly mewed. "Tell us about them."

Jane's speech locked behind closed lips. It was many moments
before she spoke. Even then she felt hemmed in, as if being devoured
by her secret. "Celeste, I'd much rather sit here with a drink or ten
and listen to how your romances unfolded. You are much more
entertaining. You are the gold standard of the trio's raw sex."

Nanette quickly agreed. "Yes. Your affairs keep us engrossed."
She scanned the menu. "They say the lobster is divine."

"It's wonderful," Celeste recommended. "I had it recently. I'll
have it, too. We sure never had lobster in Nebraska."

"I'll try the lobster," Nanette decided. "How about you, Jane?"

"I'll try to remain sane." She took another sip of her gin tonic.
To the starchy waiter, she said, "Make it three lobsters."

* * *

The gust of gossip had continued from Celeste's lips to their
ears. Jane was delighted when the tipsy Celeste ordered one more
vodka martini for the elevator, she'd laughed. She needed to be
braced between roommates on the ride to their suites. Jane and
Nanette frowned when Celeste insisted on seeing the other women's

rooms. After a quick survey of Jane's room, Celeste insisted that Jane's suite was the most elegant.

"Look, Celeste," Jane said sharply, "I'll gladly trade rooms, if that's what it takes to get you to sleep."

"Nan," Celeste slurred, "will you be a doll and get my luggage. I haven't even unpacked. I like this big suite. It has cable TV, a VCR, and all the extras." Celeste staggered, sliding down on the bed.

Jane quickly gathered her cosmetics, throwing them wildly into a bag. "My pleasure. Just don't call all night like you used to when you drank like a wino."

Packed, Jane exited. As she passed Nanette in the hall she muttered, "At least we don't have to move her."

"Good thing," Nanette replied, shaking her head. "I don't think she'd make another trip. I'd nearly forgotten how much booze she can consume."

"Oh, I left my purse on the dresser."

"I'll bring it to you after I dump Celeste's luggage," Nanette offered.

"Thanks. I'll order us a nightcap." While Jane waited for Nanette to return, she eased out of her shoes and dress. She slipped on a robe when she heard the professor return. "I thought I'd get comfy."

Nanette handed the bag to Jane. "Celeste is safely tucked in, and happy to have the best suite."

"She knows those things aren't as important to me," Jane said with a sigh. She took a melancholy plunge down on the sofa. "I'm weary but not tired enough to sleep so Celeste's suite is fine."

Nanette sat beside her. "After two and a half hours with Celeste, I'm a wreck."

"You look even more tense than I do. Need a massage?"

Magnetically, their eyes met. "That sounds heavenly. Remember when you gave me massages before finals?"

When Jane stood to answer room service, Nanette stretched out on the sofa. She turned onto her stomach. Jane placed the drinks on the coffee table. She then sat beside her ex-roommate's protracted body. "I remember. You used to get a stiff neck from studying. You're absolutely taut with strain." Jane's warm fingers delicately kneaded her shoulders.

"I'm getting more relaxed by the moment." Nanette paused. "I'm so relaxed that I may not be able to get back to my room."

"No worries, the bed is more than ample for two."

"May I ask you a question?"

"Can I reserve the right not to answer?"

"Why?"

"As you said, I'm busy with medicine," Jane said with an exasperated exhalation.

"That wasn't what I was going to ask."

"Nan, what were you going to ask?"

The moment seemed combustible. Jane's hands went motionless. Nanette turned around to face Jane. Jane withdrew her fingers when she felt the soft breasts beneath them. The heat nearly scaled Jane. Nanette didn't take her eyes from the doctor's. "You know exactly what I'm asking. Why didn't you seduce me when you had the chance?"

"The chance?" Jane repeated.

"It was when we were in the locker room twenty-six years ago. We were showering together. You touched my bare back. You nearly kissed my shoulder."

"I wanted to. Does that surprise you?"

"Why didn't you?"

Jane glanced away. "I didn't want to frighten you. The shower was slippery, and I thought you might fall."

"Why didn't you tell me how you felt?"

"Nan, I didn't want to shock you. I told you that."

"Can we return? Take that ceremonial shower together now." Nanette leaned toward Jane's lips. "If I fall, will you catch me?"

"Absolutely," Jane replied. She needn't have bothered. Their kiss answered the question. The shower was a sharing of caresses that seemed two-and-half decades late. There were amorous moments. There were moments of whimsy.

When Jane's towel-wrapped body eased into bed beside Nanette, she felt Nanette's arm slide the towel from her. Their bodies pressed, flesh to flesh, breast to breast. Warmth to warmth. Their kisses seared. Nanette's form glistened with anticipation under the low lighting. Waiting had been well worth it.

Jane's mouth swamped the professor's face with hot kisses. Their bodies corded, with Jane directing their tangle. Their skin rippled with erotic flushes as their lips explored. Love lifted them in perfect cadence. They curled, gently responding with each caress. Jane's heart raced as it had never before pounded for a woman. She'd hungered for this woman for over twenty-five years. Her cravings were now being satiated. As if locked in her throat, she muzzled her orgasmic shriek. She moaned with pleasure.

Their multi-orgasmic voyage to Lesbos had been sensually explosive, and beyond pleasurable. The solar system had been rocked off its spindle. This, both women agreed, had been the best union either had ever known. Radiant perfection, Jane had described. It was wondrous.

The women's silhouettes moved gracefully, tenderly, through the night. By morning, they snuggled with total knowledge of one another's intimacies. Nanette's face rested against the doctor's shoulder. She whispered, "I've never experienced anything like that in my life. Celeste would be shocked."

"Yes," Jane agreed. "I had a funny thought..."

"About Celeste finding out?"

"Yes. You know her husband's company is all about surveillance devices. Wouldn't it be something if she bugged this place with video and sound equipment, then suggested we trade rooms?"

Nanette giggled. "She may have needed something to pep up her alumni news." Her laughter ceased as she sat up. She scrutinized the room quickly. "Her suitcase was heavy."

Jane bolted up with a start. "You don't think she'd do that kind of thing, do you?"

"No. You're right. She isn't bright enough to set us up."

* * *

That's what they think, Celeste mused.

Just like back in college, those two were always ridiculing her. Celeste's smile swirled. She loved it. Every word was captured. Every frame of video. She would send out VCR tapes to each and every one of their classmates. Update on graduates. All the juicy updates would be unearthed. She giggled. It was so naughty.

After all, Celeste had the addresses of most of the alums. She would even have her husband's staff assist her in the tedious packaging and mailing. She watched on her small closed circuit TV. The women were cuddling into one another's curl. Oh, what they did get up to. She shuddered as she considered that it was amazing porn. Two women.

Payback is a bitch, Celeste thought. She hadn't known which of her roommates had written the words in her yearbook. One of the blondes had written it. Those dastardly words: CELESTE IS A

PUSSY PUSHOVER. Well, now was time for retribution. They were going to suffer as she had. The indignation! But now, she'd planned her *revenge*. A VCR video tape was going to be sent out to both women's families, to Jane's patients, to Nanette's fellow professors, to everyone!

Celeste watched the live camera gleefully as Nanette's fingers traced the doctor's chin. She listened in on the women's words. They were suddenly serious. Nanette said, "You know, I have been thinking about an early retirement from the university. Maybe I could move to San Diego."

"I have a better idea." Jane considered her words. "I'm tired of hiding. All these years I've been *careful*. I've got savings, investments. And I could easily sell my practice. Why don't we travel to Europe? Then decide where we want to live? It would mean we could come out."

"Come out?" Nanette snickered, "I've just barely gotten a toe into the closet and you want me to come out?"

"Hiding with a lie is the only negative about being lesbian. Think about how my chest tightened with paranoia when thinking Celeste could be bugging the place. I don't want to hide how I feel about you." Jane paused. All of her life was circumnavigating inquiries into her personal life. It was carefully weeding, extracting, or altering pronouns to conceal her precious nature. "I'm done cloaking myself. I've led a life of camouflaging. No more cryptic words. No more invisible emotions. Unveiling. That's what I'm going to do."

"Love is worth shouting about. Yes, let's come out into the sunshine."

"So even if Celeste did bug and video the room," Jane said with a laugh, "so what? It doesn't matter."

Nanette sputtered. "Even if the *pussy pushover* did try to tape us, she probably forgot to put the flipping tape into the unit."

They both howled with laughter at their joke. "She probably forgot to even buy a tape. She probably figured her servants, or Godfrey's staff, would do it for her."

Celeste's gaze left the TV screen. She quickly reached down to her VCR equipment. She frantically pressed the eject button. "Oh, shit!" she muttered to the silence.

KISS OF TIME

Autumn 2005

Strange, Hester Benson considered as she observed the neon beer sign that was still brightly lit. Through the spacious convenient store window, she viewed her lover of forty year. Beth Zered found retirement too confining. She'd taken an overnight shift at their local convenience store. Only three nights a week, but it was enough to take in a bit of socializing. Hester kept busy with her own projects. Yet she complained bitterly that she missed Beth beside her every night.

Hester noticed Beth was at the register with a customer. She scratched the buff-colored coat of their aged, shaggy, mixed breed dog. Hemingway had been rescued by the women, and he had been their constant companion. Hester often wonder if Hemingway, Hem, hadn't saved them as well. For he made them laugh. Although, Hester thought, not as much now as when he was a young dog, a decade and a half ago. Now, there was a constant list of problems. He was nearly blind, and totally deaf. His organs were beginning to deteriorate and the women seemed to be preparing themselves for the inevitable.

Hester's diminutive form bent as she tightened the lace of her walking shoe. Hem was allowed to sneak inside with her when Beth was on duty. She hated leaving him outside in the chilled San Francisco morning air.

As Hester entered the store, a gust of wind escorted them through the door. She and Hem made their way back to the cooler for cream. She wanted to fix Beth a breakfast when her shift ended in half an hour. Tucking sprays of graying, beige hair up into the knit cap that covered her ears, she glimpsed into the corner mirror. Intense powder-blue eyes stared back at her. Her oval face was kindly, pleasant, and decent. It was one of warmth and immediate recognition. Never considered a beauty, even in her youth, there was always some mystical quality about her large eyes. Her nose, mouth, and chin were tiny by comparison.

No, she thought as her image gazed back at her, she didn't look her sixty-eight years. Nor did she feel them. Both she and her lover had retired from their posts as professors a few years ago when they became eligible for retirement. Hester taught romance literature, and Beth taught astronomy. They continued to live in the campus area. That way, she contended, she was able to keep in touch with faculty and students. She wanted the continuation with academia.

Lovingly, she scanned Hem's eyes. Sixteen-years ago the women picked him up where he'd been left abandoned at the side of a road. They took him to a vet. The doctor calculated the dog to be a year or two. But Hem retained his puppy-playful spirit, even now. He tucked his body near while Hester pulled a carton of cream from the refrigerated cooler. She felt the sway of his slackened leash as they walked to the counter. Hem was beginning to get excited when Beth came into view. Hester glance down toward the dog while approaching the register area.

Her head quickly snapped upward when she heard a scuffle. Paralyzed, Hester stopped. A huge, muscular man shouted at Beth, "You tripped the alarm, bitch!" A burst of gunfire reverberated. Hester heard Beth's shriek as sparks from the gun scattered. With disbelief, Hester watched Beth's stocky frame snap backward against the rear counter. Beth crumpled, collapsing slowly to the floor. Stunned, Hester's gaze lifted to the man with the gun. When their eyes tagged, she heard a siren. "You," he motioned, spitting out commands, "get over there behind the counter. Fast, lady, or you're dead."

Beth's moan was a wringing groan of anguish. Hester began moving toward her lover. She heard Hemingway growl. With a protective stance, Hem's spate of barking provoked the man. "Hem, no," Hester yelled. "He won't bite you." She watched helplessly as the man lowered his weapon. He fired before she could continue her plea. Hemingway fell. Whimpering, his frame jerked. Hester dropped to her knees beside him. A warm rush of blood poured through her fingers. Her companion twitched several times before he expired in her arms. A swarm of tears flooded her eyes, and then drifted down her blanched cheeks.

Hester moved quickly toward Beth. She felt optimism when she saw Beth's chest expand with air. But if she were to survive, Hester realized that Beth's chest wound must be immediately treated. Her eyes pivoted back to the large, powerful, man she gauged to be in his mid-thirties. He appeared indigent, rough, and very angry. His angry eyes were scoffing. There was also indifference in those eyes that concerned Hester even more than the rage.

Her lips wobbled a heartfelt request. "My dear friend is dying. If you allow the police out there to help, they may be able to save her."

The gunman's attention was diverted back to the screeching tires in the parking lot. The squad car's blinking lights were pouring out layered colors of red and white. "She dies. So fuckin' what?" His words slashed as he seethed, "Tol' her not to pull anything. Now look what she's done to me. Your kind always looks down on my kind. I'm nothing but trash to you. I'm poor folks."

"If she dies, the charge is murder," Hester admonished. She could taste fear when she swallowed. The sourness trickled down her throat. She dared not allow her gaze to curve toward Hem. She looked only with hope upon her lover.

"Just shut up. Shut the fuck up, so I can think." He leaned his muscle-corded body back against the counter. "Yeah, or I'll shoot you, too."

Silence afforded Hester time to consider what had happened. She thought about seeing the neon sign. That should have tipped her to something being amiss. Beth was an avid energy conservationist. When the sun began its ascent, and the sky lightened, Beth always immediately unplugged the lights. She joked that burning energy might take a supernova to a white dwarf. Might cause, she teased, a gravitational collapse one day. Beth was intrigued by celestial mechanics. Also she wished to do the planet as little harm as possible.

Hester tenderly pressed a bay-colored paper towel against Beth's bleeding wound. She fought back tears. Again, she implored, "Please, her wound requires attention. Surely you don't want a murder charge."

The gunman's smug scowl of malice converted to a grin. "I been up for murder before. Somethin' always gets fucked up. Cops or court screw up, and I'm out."

"Please let her go."

"Shut up, I'm sayin' for the last time." With a sudden glower, he brandished his gun in her direction. "You bitches make me sick. You got money. I never had bucks. I had to scratch from little on. Bet you had you a nice, clean place. I come from trash."

Hester was silent. She wanted to breathe life into her lover's body. She held the towels against Beth's breastplate. She worried that her shaking hand might release even more of the oozing red liquid of life from her lover. She sensed that she was in another dimension. Her sorrow mingled with shock. This siege seemed to be impossible. Rivulets of deep crimson soaked through the towel.

Hester wished she could pull up bits of wisdom from Joubert, Apollianaire, Verlain, Rimbaud, or Dumas. She wished for comfort. Beth was struggling for breath. "Please," Hester again begged, "allow someone to help her."

"If she'da listened, she'd a been okay."

Hester began to panic. He truly hated Beth and her. She cautioned herself to reinstate calmness. She must work on bonding. For their survival might depend on that.

"What can I call you? Your name?" she asked.

"To you, I got no name. To fancy people like you, I never had no name." With a sneer, his eyes narrowed. He spat, "You ain't callin' me nothing, 'cause you're gonna keep your fuckin' mouth shut." Moving the gun, he aimed it at her. "Bang," he clamored. Then he laughed. His hoot spiraled. "Got ya. You remember that, old lady."

"This woman has never harmed anyone in her life," Hester said with a muted rage. "Please allow her to live." As if by some divine cue, Beth's breathing became a chaining fight for life. Hester's glance rotated back to her gasping lover. "Please?" Suddenly her anger and indignation surged. "You murdered an innocent pet. Now you're going to allow an innocent woman to die. How can you be so cruel?"

"You ain't seen cruel yet, bitch." He reached down to unhook the leash from Hemmingway's collar. Hester felt Beth's hand squeeze her own. Beth's eyes flickered. Hester whispered for her to hang on to life. The bullhorn call began again. The gunman's expression of defiance became pure wrath. He moved to the window, then back to Hester. He lassoed her neck with a loop of the leash and pulled her to her feet.

"How you like that, bitch?" he snorted.

Hester coughed when the leash gagged her. She was being drug in the gunman's arms toward the door. With another tug of the leash, he pressed her face against the window pane. Hester's thoughts returned to Hemingway. He'd never needed a leash, but it was required by law. He never needed to be restrained or choked. When leashed, he was always so near that the leash dangled on the ground as they walked. Such a small thing to be thankful for, Hester considered, but the fact that Hem was always free seemed meaningful. She felt the flush of cool air from a jagged hole in the glass made by a ricocheting bullet.

Bellowing through the hole, the gunman yelled, "I got hostages in here. You see this old lady. I'll kill her if you don't get me a car. Fill the gas tank. Then back off. Ya don't do as I say, and I'm killin' her."

While the police bartered, Hester watched his hostile eyes. They seemed torches of hate. When the police retreated to confer, the gunman shoved Hester back behind the counter. "Stay there or I'll put bullets in both your heads," he threatened.

Their stares confronted. Hester spat, "You're such a bitter, awful human being."

"Shut up, bitch."

Side-glancing, she saw Hemingway's body. She reached to touch Beth's face. Beth's breathing was faint. Her dark complexion, surrounded by curly salt and pepper hair, was now pale. Her touch was clammy. Beth's deep sienna eyes could out-sparkle any stars in the sky, Hester always said. Those eyes instilled a feeling of protectiveness. Those eyes were now batting, and Hester knew that a tug of war for life was going on behind the eyelids. She pressed her cheek against Beth's. "Hold on. Hold on."

Beth rallied, "Hester?"

"I'm here." Hester caressed Beth's temple She heard shouting at the window where the gunman was stationed. She leaned to whisper, "I love you, my darling."

"Over forty years," Beth sucked deeply for her next breath, "my life has been kissed by you. Thank you."

"I can't do without our kisses," Hester stressed. "Fight as you've never fought before." She gave a wink of encouragement. "Don't leave me just yet."

Beth's smile trembled. "No. Not yet. I see in your eyes that you could never do without me." Again her breathing became shallow, and she lapsed.

Hester gazed up. She saw the fierceness in the gunman's inky eyes. His glower confirmed the depth of his cruelty. "I tol you to shut up. I meant it." With a taunting, evil smirk, he issued his menacing threat. "I'll kill ya. I done it before. I raped me a couple of old ladies. Had to kill one."

Hester felt a sinking. She knew her face was paling at his confession of this heinous act. He wanted to see that revulsion. "Whatever made you bitter, your retribution is aimed at innocent people. Not the people who might have harmed you."

"Listen, bitch. You people with money and power, you only understand strength." He unfastened his jacket. His muscular chest expanded. "Got me these muscles when I was locked away." He perversely scoffed, "Your tax bucks were spent on a prison gym. So now you're learnin' about my power."

"I don't dispute your power."

"That power can kill your ass. And maybe power did kill that old broad girlfriend of yours."

"How dare you. No one has the right to harm innocent people because of the wrongs of the past. The hand dealt is never fair. But that doesn't give us the right to harm others." Hester flared. "That dog was worth a hundred of you. A thousand. When we found him, he had been brutalized. His pain didn't dim the love he gave back. That dog was smart enough to know how love begins with each new contact and each new opportunity for kindness. He didn't perpetuate unkindness by attacking innocent people."

"I jus' never had opportunity. That's what my attorneys tell the court."

"What about personal responsibility. Being responsible for your actions!" As quickly as her raw anger lurched, it was suspended. The bullhorn had taken the gunman's attention.

Scrimmaging with her thoughts, Hester reminded herself of the petition for prison rights she had signed. She had always espoused the theory of societal blame. She believed that revenge must be replaced by love. Her head sagged into her bloodied hands. She inhaled the iron scent of blood. She quickly pulled them from her face.

Sliding down, her hands reached behind her torso. She touched the contents in the space under the counter. Her fingers traced the container of scouring powder. Slowly, she eased both hands around the lid. Delicately, quietly, she lifted the lid from the tub of cleanser. She dipped her hand into the granules. Squeezing a fist full of tiny grains, she closed her eyes a moment in concentration. She now had to do whatever it might take to save them. There was little time left for Beth. It was risking everything.

She edged up, attempting to create a crouch. The gunman pivoted around to face her. He snarled, "They keep tryin' to deal me and they're gonna have a fuckin' morgue in here when I'm done." He came behind the counter and with a tug of the leash to intimidate Hester he pulled her to her feet. "They'll have themselves damaged goods. Two dead old ladies."

The scent of burnt coffee and bubble gum was so incongruous to the event. Pain was bundled inside of Hester's heart. "I would think that once you've been locked away, you'd be frightened to go back to prison."

"I'll beat it. If nobody fucks up, I may pull a few years." Scanning Hester's haggard expression, his face twisted. "It's easy to beat the system. I been doin' it all my life."

Hester surveyed Hem's body. She glanced toward Beth. Although she felt outrage, she also felt the numbness of defeat. But she held on to hope for Beth. Beth promised to hold on, and Beth had never broken a promise to her.

Her hand whirled, unfurling the cleanser into his face. When the powdery spray hit him, she screamed. With both hands, he grabbed his burning eyes. Hester heard the skittering gun as it toppled to the floor. She scurried to retrieve it. Steadying it in her shivering grasp, she aimed it at him. He re-focused his wet eyes. With waxy lashes blinking, he moved toward her.

"Stop right there," she warned. It was a challenging suggestion. Her stare followed tightly to his image. "Stop!"

"You ain't gonna shoot."

As he lunged toward her, Hester hammered her index finger against the trigger. He stumbled. She fired again. Their glare fastened. He then plummeted to the tile. She wanted her anger to dissipate. She wanted to sift the debris of her rage. Taking the leash from around her neck, she dropped it to the floor, very near his face.

Hester knelt beside Beth until the paramedics moved her. Beth was still breathing. A swarm of police entered the store. She watched as an officer reached for the gun she had been clutching. She pulled it nearer her breast, not wanting to relinquish it.

"No," her word sounded pathetic. "I might need it in case there are more bad men out there roaming the streets and hurting innocent people."

"It's okay now. We saw him leap at you. There was nothing else you could have done. He's dead." The officer comforted her. "You're safe now."

Hester's eyes watered. She watched medics lifting Beth onto a stretcher. Medics were working to save her. One yelled back that Beth would make it. A blink to the side staggered Hester. Hemingway was gone. Before she handed over the gun, she stated, "I don't believe I shall ever again be safe."

Hester was grateful that Beth would live. Also, she was

appreciative that the gunman had attempted to take the gun from her. That insured that there was no need for *her* to beat the system. Mostly she was thankful that the bullet killed the monster on impact.

She stepped over the limp body of the gunman. One of the detectives reached to steady her. When she reached Hem, she bent and whispered, "Beth is going to live. No need for you to ever worry about us again."

Hester then followed behind the gurney. She reached over as she passed by the door. Automatically, she unplugged the neon beer sign. No need to chance a gravitational collapse.

NEXT SUMMER

"Are we going to make those rapids?" one of the women questioned with a scream across the large river raft.

Dakota Goodlight watched as the ruffled waves rushed. The river was torrential. Silver-caps walloped away with increasing energy. Dakota's spirit soared. On her face was an interior smile. "Naturally," Dakota answered. And when she said the word *naturally*, it was as though some divine source of earth's primordial spirit engendered her. She was comfortable piloting the powered raft. As it rushed between the majestic sienna-red walls of the Grand Canyon, the raft lifted and swirled with the water's thrust.

This was a special passenger manifest. Thirty lesbians had booked three white water rafts. They requested all-women crews. Dakota was piloting the lead raft. She loved the fact that it had placed her among her own. It was a roster of Sapphic passengers. That delighted her.

Most of the women who had signed up for the four-day/three-night excursion were couples. But there were a few singles on the tour. Dakota hoped they all might pair up by finding that someone special on their trip.

One woman had caught her attention as they hiked the trail to meet up with the boats. The woman's light skin and auburn hair made her a sunburn candidate. Dakota's first concern was that she not be injured by the sun. Dakota cautioned the woman to make certain she used sunscreen lavishly, as well as wear her wide-brimmed Aussie hat.

Later, Dakota gave the woman some of her herbal lip balm. She noted that there was an attraction. When the woman pressed the ointment to her lush lips, Dakota swallowed her desire away. This woman might have been alone, but Dakota had a lover. She was not the cheating kind.

Dakota carefully steered the raft through the various gradient currents. She tipped back her bush-hat and gave a quick swipe across her short forehead. Long, thick, coffee-colored hair had been pulled back and tied with a woven band. She'd made that band while living on the Hopi reservation. The artistry, and her fashion, linked her tightly to her Native American heritage. From the silver and turquoise bracelet on her arm, to the knee-high moccasins she wore when they hiked, pride in her lineage was on display.

There was no denying that the twenty-six year old beauty was of Native American decent. Strong features of coppery skin, wiry muscular frame, and her quiet way, were gifts from her personal Great Spirit. Dakota's mahogany eyes seemed to communicate with nature. They also reflected her soul. A command, a laugh, and love, could be seen in those eyes. A snap of displeasure could also be measured.

The raft had been launched, and had been maneuvered through the swelling river for nearly an hour before Dakota made her self-confession. She'd been watching the woman with auburn hair. She'd even silently repeated her name several times. Jenny Davis. *Jenny*. A couple of times she'd been tagged by the lovely woman's bright jade-eyed glance in her direction. Later, there was a smile. Dakota chastised herself for looking. She sensed embarrassment from Jenny. They had both become uncomfortable with the acknowledgement of sharing that magnetism.

Running the rapids had always been thrill enough. Dakota had never paid much attention to the women who boarded her white water craft. She relegated those with any sign of affection for her to others on the tours. She wished to remain devoted. That was the nobility she expected of herself.

Dakota watched Jenny as spray hit her face. Jenny removed her sunglasses to wipe the thin bridge of her nose. Laughing, Jenny winked in Dakota's direction. A smile escaped from the young Native American's face. Dakota gulped for her next breath.

Summer river rafting trips had once assisted with tuition for Dakota's college education. The funds also came in handy for graduate school. But this summer the need for serenity had been her primary reason. It was a ritual of returning to purify her heart. Only her ancestral land offered complete peace. It was more than a getaway retreat. Here, Dakota accessed wisdom.

That was precisely why her emotions frightened her when she met the woman called Jenny. Dakota read her own feelings with great accuracy. Her gaze again became tightly ribboned to Jenny's.

* * *

"The cuisine is excellent," Jenny commented after finishing the evening meal. She hadn't expected the variety of delicious meats, fish, salads, veggies, and deserts. She had also not expected to have the feeling she was experiencing. "And I adore deserts," she chatted to the soft-spoken Native American.

"You're in excellent shape, so you don't need to watch calories," Dakota remarked.

Jenny watched Dakota stacking trays. She'd always considered love to be something other than uncontrolled hormones. Although when she and her lover, Samantha, fell in love eight-years ago, there had been unmistakable chemistry. However, it had never set off her sensory alarms. Jenny felt an instinctual desire to be near Dakota. To her dismay there was also an irresistibly sensual magnetism drawing her to the quiet pilot-guide. Jenny realized the emotion and felt a surging agony that there might be disloyalty.

Jenny quickly made reference to her lover. "I wish my mate was here. Samantha is a dancer. She's worked in film, TV, and stage. She's constantly working."

"And you?"

"I'm a florist. I have shops in New York. We live in Manhattan. That's why I thought a wilderness getaway would be wonderful." There was a pause. "One of the crew members told me that you're an archaeologist."

"Yes. My lover, Greer, is a curator. She's working on a show in Europe."

"And you didn't want to travel with her?"

"It's a very prestigious project. I'd probably just be in the way. Besides, I needed to be here this summer. And what is your reason for being away from your lover?" Dakota shyly grinned. "If I'm getting too personal, just tell me."

"Not at all. Samantha wanted to return home for a family reunion. She hadn't been with her family for a very long time, and it's going to be emotional. I thought it best she go alone. She's under so much pressure with her dancing. Her family's expectations are enormous. I guess I object to that. My parents, family, have always said to just be happy." Jenny sipped the iced tea. "To be honest, we needed to be apart for a week. That's our real reason." With a glance upward at the south-western sky's soft twilight, Jenny questioned, "And you enjoy the trips?"

"According to Hopi tradition, there is either light or darkness in your heart. At times there's a need to brighten one's heart. I needed this trip to again become exalted with life's true meaning."

"That's a reason I work with flowers and love growing plants. I belong near them."

"Yes. I think you are very much like a flower. I understand that you belong near them. Just as I belong here."

Silence pierced Jenny's heart. "There are times when I wonder where I truly belong." She didn't want to gaze back into Dakota's face. "How did you meet Greer?"

"I was finishing graduate school. I assisted with a setup of a ceremonial kiva display. Complete with kachinas."

"Dolls?"

"Yes." Dakota nodded. Her arms folded, resting against her thin frame. Jenny's face fascinated her with its brightness. The campfire gleamed against her smile. Dakota explained, "Kachinas are said to be benevolent spirits." She extended her hand in Jenny's direction. "Come on, we can climb up on the rocks. I'll show you how to view sacred sites. This is a good time because the moon is just being born for the night. Moonlight finds the sites for you. By the moon's reflection, we get a sense of our own destiny. The ledge of rock becomes the Native American's sofa. The sky is our entertainment."

Jenny felt the magic of Dakota's grasp. She hadn't wanted that softness to be so mystically wonderful. Infidelity had always been abhorrent to her. Now, she suddenly wanted this woman more than she'd ever wanted anyone in her life. Jenny questioned her own sense of destiny.

* * *

Under the great brightness of a glowing moon, a dozen women frolicked in the waters beneath a splashing waterfall. There were dozens of magnificent falls, and eddies along the river. Crew members always selected one when they docked for the night.

Women could also swim in the waters. On the first evening of traditional water play, the women wore bathing suits. But by the third and final night, most became more adventuresome, so they bathed in the nude.

Jenny had been timid the previous two nights, but Dakota had appeared sans clothing from night one. On the third night, Jenny removed her clothing so she could experience the waterfall's shower. Her nakedness was lovely, and quietly sensual.

For two days the women had shared feelings, but fought against sharing love. Each found the balance of emotions difficult. Jenny was admittedly confused. She'd never felt the humiliation of not being able to control her yearnings. The women each wanted desperately to remain monogamous. However, they were inherently aware of one another's inner struggle.

This, thought Dakota, was to be their final night together. They had shared so many words and so much warmth - without touching, there was a delicate binding of their spirits. Tonight was the final camp on this sandy river beach. Tomorrow plans were to run the few remaining miles of river, then to part. Jenny was flying back to New York to rejoin her lover. Dakota had another river trip to pilot. Greer was scheduled for Brussels where she was to lecture on 'feather offerings' of the American Indian.

Dakota watched women pairing off, going to their tents to explore romance, or just to wrap together for sleep. She and Jenny sat opposite one another on the sand. Their faces were each half in shadow and half in light. "Will you be glad to return to New York?" Dakota inquired.

Jenny's gaze lifted upward. "No. I'm frightened it will only be more of the same. This trip has made me realize that I actually resent Samantha at times. There is a constant need to prop her back up from one disaster to the next. I'm often her strength. Sometimes that makes me feel alone. Can you understand my feeling?"

"Yes," Dakota disclosed, "I love Greer, but there are incredible differences between us. Cultural. Economic. I was raised with tapestry on the walls of an adobe. Greer was raised in an opulent mansion. She'll be forty this year and she's been everywhere, and done everything, it seems. She's aristocratic, and I'm certainly not. But there is love between us."

"Samantha and I were both raised in middle-class families. And I shouldn't complain about her, but at times it's as though she doesn't even know I'm there. She is very devoted to dance. At times it's as though I'm competing with dance for her attention."

"We can talk about it. Would you like to walk to the waterfall?"

"Yes. I'll miss the evening swim and the waterfalls. And I'll miss everyone."

"I'll miss you."

Sounds of water trickling down accompanied their walk. When they reached the cascading waters, Jenny's head lowered. "I shouldn't be here like this with you. I shouldn't feel the way I do when you say things like you just said."

"Moonlight shouldn't make me this romantic, but it is," Dakota related.

Jenny turned, walking from Dakota. She waded into the shallows near the waterfall. "Coming?"

"Jenny," Dakota called as she followed Jenny under the splashing waters. "I'll truly miss you when we part."

Jenny eased back against the falling waters. The trail of water dripped in sheets down her curvy body. When she reached the fall's center, torrents of water made her slip. Dakota reached to stabilize her. Their skin contacted. With urgency, their arms wound tightly around one another.

Water pounded down. Their kiss was fire that the water couldn't seem to extinguish. Jenny felt secured by Dakota's embrace. Their deep kiss triggered their heated bodies to press even more tightly against one another.

Crashing, splashing waters became background music where each no longer felt to be a soloist in nature's symphony. They became a duet, and they knew it. Spiraling under the pouring water, their caresses continued until Jenny suddenly reeled back.

"Jenny?"

"No. I can't," she screamed. Dakota moved away. Jenny rapidly sprinted toward her tent with Dakota following. "No." she said as she turned.

"I'm sorry. What have I done?" Dakota asked.

Jenny's lips contorted. Her eyes flooded. "No, I'm sorry."

"I shouldn't have…" Dakota sucked hard to inhale. "Please, accept my apology. I'm so sorry."

"Dakota, it was my fault," Jenny sobbed. "I have never been unfaithful, but I want your love."

"I've never betrayed Greer either, and I want you. I can't explain what's happening, but can't we try to sort it out. We shouldn't part like this."

"Sort out? I want you, too. How can that be sorted?"

"We're not the straying type. I guess we don't know how to handle it. I'm awkward when it comes to social acceptances. I never know what to do, or what to say. I wasn't looking for an affair."

"I wasn't either. But I was looking for you."

"We were looking for one another. And we found each other. Maybe we need a cathartic blending and no one else will satisfy that."

Dakota sighed. "I don't know the answer for my emotions. I only know this has been the most uncontrollable force I've ever experience. I love your friendship and what we have."

"It's more than a friendship." Jenny gave her cables of damp hair a toss. She reached and took Dakota's outstretched hand. Their fingers were woven tightly for many moments. Then each woman felt the squeeze begin to release. "Why?"

"In the Hopi language there's a word for friendship – a special friend. It's *ikwatsi*.

Perhaps we do need one another. Perhaps the spirits guided us here to understand one another's needs as no one else might. Sometimes growth needs nourishment from different sources. Your plants and flowers require nourishment from more than one nutrient."

"Stay with me tonight?" Jenny invited. "We can *talk*. I've always required an explanation for each of life's events. I can't find a reason for my attraction to you."

Dakota and Jenny went to Jenny's tiny tube tent. They recognized the brevity of love. What they didn't understand was the emotion. Nor did they know what should be done about it.

* * *

Jenny had not wanted her adventure to end. Even if it had been one of the greatest mysteries - it puzzled her. The morning's ride down river allowed her to consider her feelings. Through ancient rock passageways of grandeur and romance, she had traveled. And, she considered, she had also gone through another of life's gateways. It was one that reached her interior. She searched to be healed.

She would return to Samantha a stronger person. She would again be able to provide the woman she loved with support and strength. Jenny's energy seemed restored. She was going to now be the person Samantha required. There was no question that it was Samantha's love she required. Despite everything, it was.

When they debarked, from their final leg of the trip, the two women moved toward one another. Together they had trekked the trail that was to take them back to where they each belonged. Their connection was unspoken.

"Are you going to tell Greer about our feelings?" Jenny questioned.

"Yes. She'll probably even help me work through it. Help me

understand my feelings. We'll need to examine our love. I hope it's going to make us better for one another. Are you going to tell Samantha?"

"No. I can't. It would hurt her. Artists," Jenny divulged with a hint of a smile, "are vulnerable. Dakota, although we never physically transgressed, we had strong feelings. It was an amazing attraction. An artist's ego can easily be crushed. And that would be a loss for the world. It's better that I don't mention it." Jenny's eyes closed a moment. She then examined Dakota's face. "Will you be okay?"

"Yes. Love is never disenfranchised. You'll always be in my heart."

Jenny longed to take Dakota in her arms, but dared not. She flung her backpack over her shoulder. "My *ikwatsi*. Thank you, my friend. I'm glad that we decided on friendship. I wanted you, but we both wanted our lovers more."

Dakota's smile was bright. "My special friend. Yes, *ikwatsi*."

Their hands clasped into a four-handed grasp. "Will I see you here next year?"

"I'll be here," Dakota promised. She then watched Jenny walk away.

Jenny reached the first ridge before turning back to see Dakota. She hadn't expected a return wave. But she got one. Dakota then gathered her gear and considered the length of a year.

Dakota had never been tempted. Her smile felt correct. Had this happened to test her? Maybe. Had it been because the goddesses wished to strengthen her? Perhaps. Was it a spirit guide tricking her? Possibly.

All that she completely understood was that one episode in life became miscued. Or it could have been that her soul lost its voice. Her spirit had wrestled. That she knew for certain.

She was also now aware that she could resist temptation.

Photograph by Kathie Solie

NO-FRILL LOVIN'

"Well! Wouldn't that just stew a button?" Zelda exclaimed.

"Whatever are we going to do?" Queenie's concerns spurt through her trembling lips with a panicked urgency. "We'll freeze to death in here." Her eyes roamed the dim lit walk-in refrigeration storage cooler.

"First of all, I'll turn the thermostat down as far as it will go." Zelda went to the small enclosed box. She opened it, gave a twist to the dial, and then pressed the door shut again. "There." She rapidly glanced back at Queenie. "Good thing we were ready to lock up the restaurant. At least we have our coats on." Still holding the bottle of champagne she'd carried when they entered the refrigeration unit, she lifted it. "All I wanted to do is show you the exact spot where champagne best chills. It was my fault for not watching the door. I should have checked the latch. I'd forgotten it hasn't been repaired yet."

"What about air?" Queenie lowered her torso down onto the edge of a milk crate.

"There's plenty. It's spacious in here. And," Zelda stated confidentially, "the pantry women will be on duty in an hour or two." She sat on a nearby crate. "What we need to do is keep our bodies activated. For warmth."

"Yes," agreed Queenie. Her head ticked up and down in total accord. "We must try to stay warm."

Zelda, the restaurant hostess, had always executed the seating of patrons with perfect attention to detail. She was certain Queenie wondered how it was possible that she'd made this major blunder. Zelda, with her disciplined, composed personality, could also be jovial. But often, when directing the waitresses and busboys, she displayed a stern, businesslike attitude. She was not the type of person to make a mistake of this magnitude. Especially allowing the cooler door to shut and incarcerate them.

By Zelda's own self-description, she was a tad tubby, with dyed brunette hair and chocolate eyes that snapped with humor or anger. In her early forties, she'd always carefully planned each phase of her life. Just the way she meticulously planned the dinner-rush seating. She always perfectly stacked the book-menus like a deck of cards.

But Zelda had no clue about Queenie's personality. The enigmatic newest recruit in the army of serving staff had captivated Zelda's imagination. Queenie was a tad too bony. In her late-thirties, Queenie was called a 'highfalutin bitch' by her fellow employees. She wore her straw-blonde hair in a well-wrapped braid on her head. Ice-blue eyes dutifully quashed passes made by overly friendly restaurant patrons. She bragged that she only dated *true professionals*. But, Zelda noted, Queenie was always first to volunteer for Saturday nights. Other serving staff called Queenie a frost princess. But Zelda bet that was not the case.

Zelda looked around at the neatly stacked canisters, and crates. She suggested, "Let's make it as comfortable as we can. That's the least we can do while we're stuck in here." She gathered a drop cloth from the floor. She carefully spread it over a long double row of sturdy crates. Then she placed a large packing pad atop the cloth. "Makes a nice little blanket to sit on. There." She sat and patted the space beside her.

"Just sit yourself right down here and we'll have a little talk."

Queenie slowly eased onto the crate. "It's always good to get off my feet."

"Do you enjoy being a waitress?"

"Oh, yes. It takes time to make friends though. I don't think the others like me."

"Queenie, it will get easier for you."

"They think I'm too prim and proper."

"Yes. Well, since we're here, we might as well break open the bubbly." Zelda popped the champagne cork with flourish. With a quick gulp, she shook her head. "Normally, I wouldn't dare drink on the job. But as we're here. This situation does call for a little bracer." She handed the bottle to Queenie. "Go on, you need a little nip of courage."

Queenie clutched the bottle. Then with a giggle of embarrassment, she pressed the bottle to her lips. "Umm, very good year." She examined the label. "Maybe the champagne will warm us."

"Yes. And as you say, it is an excellent year. Glad I selected it and didn't pick up one of those ratty cheap bottles."

"Do you think the other girls will eventually accept me?"

"Of course, dear." Zelda issued a flashing smile. "Why just in the last few minutes I've gotten to know you better." Several sips later, she continued. "And I do like what I see."

Queenie flushed. "My goodness. I though you disliked me even more than the others."

"Not at all, dear."

"I do hope we won't freeze to death just when we've become friends."

"Not to worry," Zelda reassured her. "We're in what you might call a controlled environment. Granted, we'd be far better off if we were seals," she added with a chuckle. Her arm bridged with Queenie's when she passed the bottle back.

Queenie echoed her with her own titter. "Yes, we're in a bit of a pickle. I'm already feeling chilly. Do you truly think we'll be okay?"

"We'll be fine." Zelda reinforced her words with a confident, firm series of pats on Queenie's shoulder. When her hand dropped, she brushed Queenie's arm. "You are cool to the touch. We don't want frostbite. To safeguard, perhaps we should bundle together. Conserve heat."

"Bundle? Together?"

"Yes," Zelda's arm eased around Queenie.

Fitting into the crook of Zelda's embrace, Queenie snuggled. "That is better."

"Of course it is, dear. But I have another suggestion. Perhaps if we took off our coats, we could lie down so that the full length of our bodies will share heat. Our coats can be used as covers."

As instructed, Queenie removed her coat. She slid between the wall and Zelda's outstretched body. Recumbent, they pulled their coats over them. "That's much warmer."

Feeling the heat, Zelda concurred. She brushed a spray of curls from Queenie's forehead. "Better. But it's becoming a virtual blizzard of cold in here."

Queenie's teeth began chattering. "I just don't know what else we can do."

"Our only chance for survival might be rather unconventional. Now, I've heard tell that there is one way to stay perfectly warm. An old wives tale perhaps. But they say that the most intense heat a body produces is with orgasm."

"I...." Queenie stammered, "I'm...not...not sure how....."

"Where there's a will, there's a way," Zelda offered. "We could always make an attempt." She snuggled near as she crept toward hormone heaven. "Why don't I try to satiate you - in that way?" With great dexterity, Zelda's hand pried between Queenie's legs. She slipped their skirts upward. Gently, skillfully, she eased her body over Queenie. "Yes," she murmured, "this just might be the ticket." Her sturdy body began to rock. She continued. Their skin coiled together as their frames heaved with waves of passion. Soon Zelda felt sweat pouring over her temples.

"Oh, yes," cried Queenie. She was no longer shivering. She sizzled with sparks of heat. Her hips twisted beneath Zelda. "I'm burning up," she reported through clamped teeth. "Yes. Yesssss."

Zelda plunged against Queenie. She was considering that not one of her fellow employees would ever believe this scene. Prim and proper. Huh! With legs flying in the air like distress flags, Queenie was aflame with sensuality. Zelda felt her own teeth grind when her orgasm overwhelmed her. She heard a moaning cry of joy from the ice princess when Queenie climaxed.

After regaining her composure, Zelda shared, "Well, Queenie, I do believe there's something to that theory. I'm positively hot as a pistol now."

"Me, too," Queenie agreed. She fought for scraps of breath. "It certainly did the trick."

"Didn't it just," Zelda ratified. She sat up, patting her skirt down. She threw her hands to her face. "Oh, my! I just thought of something." She went to the control panel box. "I almost forgot about the safety latch inside here. It's a manual latch somewhere. Here we go." With a flick of her finger, she heard the cooler door groan open.

"Thank goodness!" shouted Queenie. "You are such a hero in all this. I believe you've saved our lives."

"It was all in the line of duty, dear." Zelda flung the squashed bundle of mats and cloth from the crates. "The important thing is that we're safe."

"We are." Queenie gave Zelda the cool kiss of a distant relative on her cheek. "And I'll be home before my late night soap opera comes on TV."

"I'm so very glad." Zelda gave motion for Queenie to leave. "I'll finish locking up. I don't want you to miss out on your story."

"I try never to miss an episode." She turned when she reached the door. "Again, thank you so very much. You're a brick. An absolute brick."

"Don't mention it, dear," Zelda watched as Queenie exited. She turned back around to make certain the cooler was in order. She pitched the empty champagne bottle in the trash.

She then smiled. Remarkable, she mused. No-frills seduction, but it never failed.

PIONEER *JOIE de VIVRE*

The fateful decision was ultimately in Catherine's lovely hands. As was my captive heart.

Remembering back three years, in 1893, I recalled her as she proceeded from the train's steps. Prairie Center, Kansas, was expecting the arrival of our new school teacher. Surely, I considered as I glanced at the small station's platform, this regal, elegant, and certainly lovely woman could not be Catherine Foster. But she was the only woman alone. She was also surveying the area. Our eyes met.

She daintily lifted her long, billowy skirt, showing just enough of her petticoat as she walked toward me. Perfectly corseted, her small waist and lifting bosom were far too Eastern Coastal. Bostonian, perhaps. But this was the Great Plains. She was, I thought as my lungs expelled a soft gush, far too sophisticated and refined.

Catherine was in perfect vogue. Shining pearl buttons lined her bodice. Her puffed leg-of-mutton sleeves gave a fashionable lift to her shoulders. Although her bone structure was delicate and tiny, she had the spirited prance of a thoroughbred. That proud carriage went well with her wide-brimmed royal blue hat. Her bonnet was beribboned with flowing sunshine-colored streamers.

When her long-lashed eyelids shyly dipped, a quiet innocence was portrayed. Blue, those eyes were, with vibrancy. A radiance the likes of which I've never before seen; or known. Honey-hued curls spilled down from beneath her bonnet - down from their high piling that was anchored with a mother-of-pearl comb.

How I *did* fall in love with her that very moment.

When I reached to take her valise, her gloved hand brushed mine. We strolled to my awaiting horse and carriage. With a fright most foreign to me, I introduced myself. "I'm Sarah Lind, Miss Foster."

"Please call me Catherine. Miss Foster is how my classroom pupils address me." Her smile was virtually brilliant.

"Catherine," I said. My lips warmed to the word. "Catherine, welcome to Prairie Center. I do hope you'll enjoy your stay at Lind

Boarding House. We'll do everything possible to make you comfortable."

"I've never been West before," she divulged as we walked. "It's very rugged."

"Yes," I spoke with a laugh. "I felt the same way when I moved here from Albany three years ago. I was exactly your age, twenty-two, when I arrived. The boarding house was my inheritance from a maiden aunt. I'd planned to sell out and return East. But I came to feel very much at home here. I'm now at ease in my small western town."

"It is," she paused, filtering words, "very rural."

"It isn't as rip-roaring as you might believe," I playfully teased. "There are occasional barroom brawl, a shootout or two, and from time to time an Indian raid." When her eyebrows lifted in alarm, I laughed. "Actually, our tornadoes are the most excitement we have here."

"But you do have cyclone cellars?" she asked with concern.

"Yes. We'll keep our schoolmarm safe. Don't you worry about that." I automatically reached to pat her arm. "You have my word, your security is most important to us all."

As months passed, Catherine's well-being became even more vital to me - to my life. After finishing lunch at the boarding house, I often took steaming hot buttermilk biscuits to the schoolhouse. Wrapped neatly in gingham towels, the biscuits were a treat for the twenty-six schoolchildren. An accompanying large pot of honey seemed to be a true favor for the children. The sweetness was generously drizzled on each biscuit served.

Once, after the children were released for recess, Catherine and I stayed behind. She lifted a well-doused biscuit and playfully aimed it for my mouth. When it pressed between my lips, my limbs went weak. She shyly smiled when I nodded my approval. Then we laughed. Her laugh, well, I had fallen in love with that laugh. The laugh and the lady.

I watched Catherine as a teacher. At her blackboard, she pointed out spelling and grammar errors with grace and kindness. I don't believe she ever once raised the paddle that hung from a wall nail. She encouraged each child to read, and to think. Many students borrowed her books to read by buffalo-tallow candles that lighted their sod homes. Catherine allowed *McGuffey's Readers* to become the children's dear friend.

Our friendship grew. I watched Catherine as a woman, as well as an educator. We strolled the creek's banks, gathered wildflowers, and even fished. We discussed events of the day, the fiction of the past, and we laughed about the frivolities in life. We loved our outings.

After several months, our bond had deepened. The evening I knew of my desire was when she called out to the hallway from the bath. She had forgotten a towel. I retrieved one from the linen closet. Slowly I entered the steaming bathroom. She was immersed in foamy suds. The scent of bath crystals merged with the fragrance of pink geraniums on the window sill.

"Here's the towel," I spoke softly as I placed it beside the tub. My eyes diverted from her lovely ivory body. Her lips mouthed a thank you. "Your wish is my desire."

"My wish is to have my back scrubbed." Her words were teasing - yet innocently spoken.

"I would be most *happy* to scrub your back."

"I like it when you're *happy*."

"Catherine, you do make me happy. And I would be most happy to bathe your back. Your neck." I was thinking each word, for each portion of her.

She threw the washing cloth in my direction. With a laugh, she leaned forward. I sat on the tub's side. My hands trembled. I dared not allow my fingers to touch her skin. With cloth carefully beneath them, I tenderly washed her back.

Then she moved ever so slightly. My hand brushed her neck. I pushed the spray of her curls upward. Her face turned. My eyes were fixed upon her. Then my hand reeled away quickly. My cheeks burned with the realization that I wished to touch her in a loving way. For several moments I stalled, unable to move. Then my gaze was broken. "Your back is officially well-scrubbed."

"Thank you, Sarah."

I stood. My knees felt nearly too weak to carry me, but carry me they did. When I shut the door behind me, I leaned back against it for many moments. The few splashes I heard suddenly stopped. I heard her sobbing. How I did want to go to her. I wanted to apologize for any brashness, or yearning she may have seen on my face. I chastised myself. I then went to my bed. Tears poured from my eyes. I would never hurt her for the world. Yet I was certain my craving must have been read by her insightful eyes.

Curling into a miserable fist-like ball, my body shook with tears so silent and so desolate, I feared for my next breath. And yet, the heart that beat so boldly, that soared with such lofty exaltation for those moments, was now breaking as crystal upon stone.

My longing was wicked. It was but a footnote in history's hidden archives. It was scarcely hinted at throughout the century.

For many days my eyes evaded her glances. As, perhaps, she was eluding mine.

* * *

In my loneliness, dredging memories was difficult. But those recollections were all that remained. Love was beneath the surface. Well out of the way, until one afternoon changed everything. It was a cloud-shaded Saturday in summer. Catherine had agreed to teach some of the Russian children in a village two miles out of Prairie Center. The livery stable gave her the use of a horse so that she might ride to a sod cabin where the children gathered each Saturday. There she taught a handful of eager students.

By mid-afternoon, I became concerned. The skies were filled with huge, frightening black clouds. I recognized their undersides. The storm was howling. It was hanging over the exact area when Catherine was. Unable to confine my fear, I rushed to bridle and saddle my horse. I might be able to reach her before the storm. I'd warn her to seek shelter in the dugout.

As I rode, I felt the dust and grit gathering in my mouth and throat. In front of me was a dark mass of dirt. The funnel-shaped cloud approached. I feared I might be too late. Then I heard her call my name.

Dismounting, I called to her. "Catherine, Catherine!"

"I'm here." Her arms reached for mine.

In my embrace, she shuddered. My eyes burned from the dust. I asked, "Are the children safe?"

"I sent them home earlier."

"But why didn't you stay there in the safety of the dugout?"

"Sarah, I had to warn you. The storm was heading toward you. It's going toward Prairie Center." Her words rushed. "I don't know what I'd do if anything happened to you." Her hands reached and softly caressed my cheeks.

I looked up to see the deadly twister bearing down on us. I swatted our horses, and they wisely galloped toward home. Without a rider's weight, they would surely be able to outrun the storm and make it to safety. Their return to the stable, I reckoned, would alert the town-folk to search for us.

With Catherine's hand in mine, I began running. "We must make it to the ditch. Over there, that ravine," I instructed.

As we reached a dip in the land, I pulled her down. We rolled into a place where the earth was deeply indented. Her body pressed mine. Her arms wrapped around me. I felt the heat as her breasts crushed against my own. Her lips brushed across my cheek and then rested against mine. Her heart pulsed with urgency and fear. When our kiss ended, I felt a love so grand that it was impossible to ignore. We did not ignore it. We would not ignore it.

The very earth had moved beneath us. The great and grandiose plains had been battered and beaten by torrents of winds. All around us, the skies swirled. All had been pounded and twisted.

That afternoon, we had survived a deadly tornado in our efforts to warn one another. We had also survived love's truth.

Joy had entered my heart's home.

* * *

Now, joy might be leaving me forever. Recalling my French tutor back in Albany, I felt some portion of a lullaby. My teacher had related that love often meant allowing another freedom to take leave. She had shared pleasure with me when I was eighteen. But she had made me aware that lovely young women need to settle down. Women marry and produce a family. But while it was there, love, as life, should insist upon *joie de vivre*.

This I had told Catherine the first night we spent in one another's caressing embrace. It would be joy for that moment. Then we must let go with love. A woman must be socially acceptable.

Why was it now difficult to accept that Catherine had believed those words? I had encouraged her. I had sent Daniel Woodrow's attention to Catherine. I even took her on that picnic. It was meant to allow her the freedom of selecting. It was meant to hearten her decision.

That picnic. Her words were warm. "Sarah, what are you pondering? I don't believe you've said two words all the way out here," Catherine said.

I glanced around at the isolated picnic area we'd chosen for our treasured time away from our responsible lives. It was within a grove of oak trees near a brook. Waters gurgled, singing to us.

My head rested in her lap. I smiled. "I was thinking about how perfect this getaway is. The day is absolute perfection." My arms swayed the panorama of a vast horizon. "All the day is our perfection."

"It isn't perfect at all." She leaned over me. Her breasts lingered over my face as she reached toward the picnic basket. She retrieved a fried chick leg. "Here," she directed as she ushered the drumstick in my mouth. "Maybe food will improve your misery."

I laughed as I munched. "Darling, please, we must relax so we might *enjoy* our day." I shared the drumstick with her. "It's magnificent out here. And you are most lovely of all." I leaned back. Grasses beneath the gingham checked cloth were soothing. The day was meant to be a time of sharing happiness.

"How on earth can I enjoy the day," she said with a sad and sullen voice.

"Whatever do you mean?"

"You don't seem to mind that Mr. Woodrow is courting me."

"Catherine, my sweetheart, you're very young. You have the rest of your life before you. I want you to have respectability. I would hate to see you grow old without a family. You would become known as a spinster teacher."

"That doesn't bother me," Catherine alleged with a pout. "I truly love you, Sarah. I don't know why respectability need be so complicated."

"Most women's lives are authenticated through marriage. A family. Children. A home life. I don't want my love for you to spoil that opportunity."

"You sound like my parents. And the women in the church. They say that I'm getting older, and must secure my future. They say a proposal doesn't come along every day."

"And so it does not." I inhaled deeply - painfully. "Mr. Woodrow is respected. He is wealthy. He can give you everything. Respectability. Security. Family life. All the things I can never give you."

Catherine's back went stiff. "But I love you." Her hand glided my face. "I do love you," she repeated. "I love your bronze, silky curls, and the way they fall across my body as we share love. I adore your green eyes and their sparkle. I also am intrigued by the softness of your smile. I do so love your homespun tales. You make me laugh." She paused. Her head dipped. "When did you first know you were in love with me?"

"From the moment I first saw you. I have always been in love with you, Catherine." My gaze escaped hers. "And do you recall your first feelings for me?"

"Indelibly. Yes. You were playing the parlor piano, and we were singing. Our eyes met. When we both reached to turn the sheet music, our fingers brushed. I felt my own hand trembling. Even as I fiddled with my demitasse cup there was a quaking inside that remained. Our glance also continued. I wanted you to bundle me in your arms."

"That was so long ago. When you first arrived."

"I have loved you that long. Yes."

I closed my eyes. I considered all the nights of listening for her timid wrap on my door. How our fondness turned to fervent love. Her sheltered ways had endeared her to me. She was a bouquet of wild flowers. I had gathered those flowers to my heart.

I suddenly wanted to weep for love of her. I was glad when I heard the horse snort. He was still harnessed to the buggy that was hitched to a tree limb. For each quiet pause created a pain the likes of which I'd never known.

I looked longingly into Catherine's rapturous face. "I want your happiness," I whispered. "Above all, I want that. And it must be your decision. Mr. Woodrow has been patient for most of the year. But he wants your answer about a future with him. He deserves that. He is a fine gentleman," I spoke, attempting to mask the melancholy from my voice.

"I don't know why he's so insistent on an answer tomorrow."

"Perhaps Mr. Woodrow needs reassurance." At times, I considered, Catherine's slight frown made her face look so like a painting. An image more wondrous than any I knew. Her smile was poetry. And of course, her voice was music. She was my heart's visit with creative artistry

"I could never love him as I love you."

My emotions were being roused by the conviction in her voice. But I muzzled my feelings. I opened the picnic basket. I broke a crimped edge from our cherry pie. Then I slipped it between her sensual, soft lips.

My appetite was dulled with the thought of Catherine's become a dutiful wife. I could never imagine her wanting to quench a man's passion. My eyes cast downward. Even my locket held one of her golden locks of hair. No, I shant think of her with another. But I must. For her sake, I argued. My eyes scolded her. My voice was resolute.

"Catherine, should you decide to consider marriage, you must forget all that we've shared."

"Our love is written on my spirit. Sarah, I can never forget. I don't understand why we must hide such loveliness."

"It's considered to be against nature. Perhaps one day the fineness of our love will be understood. Perhaps it will even be accepted. Maybe one day women with our desires will be free to openly express themselves. But this is not the time."

With exuberance, she agreed, "Yes, one day it may be accepted. Why women might even have their very own places to meet one another. Clubs. Salons, like in Europe. Perhaps in the future women will be able to raise children together. Or marry."

"But not now," I purposely negated her dream.

"But one day. Why there's Elizabeth Cady Stanton. I've read her works in old volumes of *Revolution*. My aunt had saved them from her own youth in 1870."

"You've read the militant women's rights magazine?"

"Yes," she declared proudly. "While I was back East, I followed the various promotions of the National Women Suffrage Association. And Susan Brownell Anthony is fighting for the rights of women. Just a few years ago the International Council of Women was founded. Strides are being made for women."

"Women. Not women like us."

"All women. We are women first. And you can't deny there is a possibility that one day we shall have a forum."

"Sadly, all that is possible is in the distant future. Far away from today. We must be resigned to live in today's world," I lamented. "I can't give you children, an acceptable home, nor can I give you respectability."

"I have my pupils. The boarding house has been the most wonderful home I've ever known. And there is no human being I more respect than you." With the tip of her head, she added, "So there."

When I began a rebuttal, she pushed a savory portion of chicken toward my open mouth. By the time I swallowed, we were both laughing. "Catherine, you never want for answers. I *do* love your sass."

"I *do* love you, Sarah."

"If you love me, consider your decision carefully. It is for the good of your future."

Her eyes dimmed momentarily. She looked away, facing great

chalky bluffs to our East.

* * *

Catherine retreated to her own thoughts.

Abandoned in my solemn, goose-down, four-post bed, I wept. For we had determined it was best for Catherine to spend the night in her room. She needed time to consider her decision. That was my time to reconcile myself to never again hearing her knock at my door. Our tightly-bound bodies would never again glow with the luster of love. I would no longer be wrapped in the sheen of her. Moonlight was never to spill across our bodies. My warmth was never again to be.

Catherine would be mollycoddling her husband. Pampering him and loving him. She'd become busy with children and church functions. She would take her happiness to a fine, large home. She could fill that home with her smiles, her laughter, and her dreams.

Tears streamed, skimming my flushed cheeks. I stared at the dim glimmer cast by my kerosene lamp. Strange bars of light were reflecting through the back of my rocking chair. They sketched a prison against the wall. Catherine's nightgown was not resting in the lap of that chair. Nor was she in my arms. Our flesh was not tightly strapped to one another's.

The world appeared incorrect.

I began to bury my face in the pillow when I heard a knock on the door. I sat up. Grabbing for my robe, I considered it must be one of the boarders. Or perhaps it was fate tricking me with the want of Catherine. Again, the faint wrapping against my door was heard.

"Yes," I called out. "Who is it?"

"Sarah, I must talk with you" Catherine's words were troubled.

I scurried to the door and flung it open. Her eyes were damp. She moved past me, quickly. She sat in the rocking chair. I closed the door, and then returned to the bed's edge. Slowly, I sat. She reached for my hand. Clutching it tightly, she grasped it has she never before had. I asked, "Catherine, what's wrong?"

"I must ask a question of you. You must promise me the truth. I must know your own sweet heart-truth."

"You have my word."

"Sarah, when I talked with you about marriage to Mr. Woodrow, you weren't upset. I must know how you truly feel. Are you behaving indifferently to his proposal because of what you believe to be unselfish motives? Or is it that you no longer care for me in the way you once did?"

"My darling," I lulled, hushing her sobs. I eased down onto my knees before her. My head fell into her lap. "I'm not indifferent to your love. I only want what's best for you." My kiss grazed her hand. "I adore you. More now than ever."

"Then why are you sacrificing me?"

"Sacrificing you? I'm in love with you. You mean the world to me." I felt her fingers on my head. Caressing me. Fondling my curls. "I didn't want to make an attempt to sway your decision. I don't want you to ever regret our love."

"I have never regretted a moment of loving you; nor have I regretted your love for me."

"I wanted your decision to be unencumbered by my emotions for you." Words had been stopped in my throat. My pause was one of searching out the next thing I might say. It couldn't be lacking. It couldn't be selfish.

"My decision is made."

Catherine slowly stood. She helped me to my feet and into her embrace. I followed her to our bed.

"I am your decision?" I questioned.

She whispered, "There are worse things than being called a spinster schoolmarm.

But for the life of me, I can't think of one thing worse than living without you."

"You'll be staying on?"

"I'll be spending my life here. Sharing *joie de vivre* with the woman I cherish above all others. Does that meet with your approval?" Her lips curled sweetly.

"That woman of whom you speak," I replied with a smile on my heart. "That woman is the most grateful pioneer on the frontier."

ROARIN' RASCALS

Helen took her place in the best chairs, at the finest tables, in the most prestigious gourmet restaurants. Seating for royalty, was hers – not only in New York – but in every major city. Money counted as much as charisma, she'd learned from an early age. From the best seat in the house she experienced the finest panorama of Jazz Age personage - the famous and the infamous. She witnessed the Roarin' Twenties society in motion – in full roar.

Behind Helen's spectacles were pale green eye-vaults. Her eggshell-white teeth shone when her lush, sensual lips formed a smile. As if pulling a curtain, those lips created an instant grin or a full pout. Helen was wearing an aristocrat's golden sun-kissed skin. It fit her tradition and her elegantly athletic walk. Her casual stroll was automatic, effortless. And that glide was accentuated by her clothing selection. Elegant wools, in rich colors, blended with her Riviera tan.

Carefully styled, her chestnut-colored hair was not bobbed, nor was it long. Overt fads were not her style. She was never to be mistaken for a Flapper, so short skirts were considered a frivolous craze. No matter, there was still a bit of a rebel. Helen often balked against her staunch and sedate family. Objectionable to her family were trousers. Trousers were one of her very favorite fashions to wear. She often wore a checkered pair with matching tailored jacket. A felt, helmet-formed hat swirled above her right forehead. Fashionably tipped, it showed her face off to great advantage. She never needed thigh-high skirts to give her a sexy style. For that, at least, her parents were pleased.

Although her mother expressed disdain over her panted daughter, Helen explained that she wasn't looking for a husband. She was merely meeting up with alma mater chums. Her mother, most often, acquiesced. If only sorority sisters were there, no need to show off Helen's well-proportioned body.

However, Helen was considered dowdy by one of her ex-roommates. Trixie made every attempt at updating poor Helen. She often, according to Trixie, looked as if she lived out of a dreadful rucksack. Trixie's own yellow-blonde hair was bobbed to precision. It included a spit curl. Trixie was up-to-date in every sense of the word. Her own pastel-blue eyes appeared painstakingly painted by cherubs. Helen referred to her glamour gaze as an eyes-in-the-headlight look.

Trixie's thin, petite form was always dressed to the nines. Her vamp outfits, she called them. And she wished Helen would take her recommendations to select a Parisian designer or two. Trixie swore by them. But her suggestions were to no avail. Rather than thanks, Trixie only received Helen's visual reprimand.

Helen glanced up from the chic restaurant's best table in the tearoom. Trixie was strutting toward her with trend-setting aplomb. She leaned across the table to greet her chum with a quick kiss on each of Helen's cheeks. She then plunged into her chair. "Helen, darling."

Helen gave her smudged cheeks a wipe with the napkin before acknowledging Trixie with a nod. Trixie was wearing at least half a tube of lipstick for the occasion, Helen thought. And Trixie's skirt was so short that it did more than expose her silk stocking wrapped legs. With great flamboyance, Trixie patted down the hem that kept her garters from showing.

"Trix, dear."

"Helen, you really are due for a haircut. Do try that new salon. It would offer a world of good for you."

Helen smiled. "I may be due for a trim, but you certainly aren't. If they lift any more from your crown, you'll be positively bald."

"It's slickened down. That's the thoroughly modern way." Trixie giggled. She had poured a crystal flacon of perfume over her nimble torso. "My spirit is positively receding to gloom. I'm sagging after the long trip home."

"I'm amazed that you've returned from Europe so soon. New York is no replacement for Paris. We haven't the perfume." Helen inhaled deeply. "Wearing something new?"

"Yes," Trixie answered coyly. "It's called 'Bubbly Butterfly.' I simply love trying new scents."

"I know you do. So why *did* you return?"

"Daddy insisted I come back for my brother's wedding. What a bore. An absolute bore! I've been on the trot since I arrived. The week has ravaged me," she complained through her slack-jawed, Eastern finishing school intonation. "And you're looking marvelously tanned, kiddo. Your makeup could use a bit of work, but what a lovely bronze you're sporting."

"Thanks. I used a beautician located in the center of a nether world," Helen reported with a laugh. "Actually, I smeared some paint across my mug, and that's that."

"Yes." Trixie gave a hearty sigh of agreement. "I was a tad late. I'd hoped that

Glynis was going to be on time." She scanned the tearoom's vista. Sucking in her rosebud lips, she added, "She's always been tardy."

"Tardy?" Helen was amused.

"Yes. Most unpredictable."

"Ah, yes. *Unpredictable*. But I find that is part of her charm. So, Trix, how was Europe?"

"Flaming youth! Oh, Helen, the men are so divine. Golly, but they are romantic."

"It must have been difficult to leave all that romance behind."

"Yes. Like a weepy at the flickers. And sadly, I needed to return to this Philistine civilization. Gosh, but I do miss European men."

Dryly Helen inquired, "Did you do any sightseeing?"

"There's bags of time left in life for that kind of thing. I needed to experience the real world. I'm collecting the truly cherished events of life. Moderation doesn't exist in Europe. Now that I'm back in the land of Prohibition, I realize how liberating Paris is."

"Prohibition doesn't mean a thing."

"Too right it doesn't. Golly, I do love the intrigue of speaks. I've been to a speakeasy nearly every night this week. It's all so perfectly sinful," she divulged with a bat of her eyes. She whispered, "Illicit intoxicants actually taste much better, don't you think."

"Better than what?" Helen teased.

"Silly girl! You know what I'm saying."

"*You* can never be certain what you're saying, so why should I be? But do elaborate." Helen's amusement placed a lift on her lips.

"The Jazz Age. Excitement. All that *complete* fire of life. I swear, on a good night I feel as though fireworks are exploding inside. This age is thrilling beyond compare. Henry Chase III told me that my jigglers are two in a million," she sputtered. "That's something my mother wouldn't have heard at a cocktail party. The women on French beaches don't wear halters. *Nothing*. I swear."

"Perhaps I'll plan a little trip later this year," Helen teased.

"Oh, Helen, you would never go without a top."

"I might. One deserves a thrill or two while one is still above ground."

"Parisian men are so thrilling. Positively everyone on the continent owns a roadster. Romance is forever in the air."

"According to Freud, romance is mostly libido," Helen observed.

"Well, there's plenty of that going on in Rome."

"Rome is the city of clinches and pinches."

"Umm, galore!" Trixie half hummed. She surveyed the length of the approaching waiter's body. "Tea and crumpets," she ordered without glancing at the menu. "Oh, no. They're so British. Finger sandwiches might be nice. And tea."

"Make that three," Helen said. "We're expecting a friend soon."

When the waiter was out of hearing range, Trixie confided, "Now, he might make a wonderful lover."

"If…?"

"If he were rich he'd be in contention." Trixie gave a flirty laugh. Her eyes were fiery. "I'm delirious when I reach that point of no return. So I must take finances into consideration up front. You know what a good man can do for you."

"I know what a great lover can do for you. I have been around the world a time or two. There's nothing like a lavish affair in the low-rent district of Paris."

Trixie giggled. "Yes. The only place where men are scarce is the Alps. It's turning into the *Swish* Alps, if you get my drift." She twirled her long strand of pearls. "There's such an awfully lot of *that kind of thing* going on these days."

Helen glance way. With a chuckle, her resonant voice agreed. "Isn't there just?"

The women watched Glynis approach their table. Glynis, with her dark auburn hair, warm topaz eyes, and flashing smile, always gleamed with mystery. She possessed a warmth that both of her friends admired. Her only fault, Trixie had often mentioned, was that Glynis was from *fresh* money. Her father had made his own millions.

Perhaps, Helen always countered, that was what made Glynis so refreshing and so poised. And what enabled the lovely Glynis to converse with such ease in any social stratum. As Glynis sat, she bantered with the waiter about his perfect timing. Tea was delivered within moments of her arrival. But, she questioned, is the tea *tainted*?

The waiter chuckled, and then replied that there were no alcoholic additives.

"He must think you're insane," Trixie scolded. "Honestly, Glyn. I brought my silver flask, but now he'll probably be watching us."

"If he's watching us, it isn't because of what we drink," she replied.

"So pull out your flask," Helen passed her cup in Trixie's direction. "Pour me a double or I'll report you to your mother immediately."

"If only my mum could see me now," Trixie blurted as she unscrewed the cap of her flask. "She is a charter member of the Woman's Christian Temperance Union! Thank goodness Daddy isn't such an old stitch. This is from Daddy's private reserve." She poured heartily.

Helen sipped. "Umm, Yummy. Certainly not bathtub gin."

"Does Daddy know you're tapping his still?" Glynis questioned.

"Of course not. You know Daddy. He believes I'm a child. He calls the Charleston a vulgar mating dance."

"He *is* an old stuff shirt," Glynis joked.

"He gave me a dog for my birthday," Trixie reported.

Glynis and Helen traded glances. Helen felt Glynis' hand under the table. The fingertips crawled gently to Helen's knee. "Razz-ma-tazz!" Helen whispered. Her skin heated as she shuddered. "I don't want a bitch for my birthday," she said with a deep laugh. "But I know who I do want."

Trixie frowned. "You birthday is not until next month, you silly girl. And my dog is *not* any such thing as a bitch. I call her Fluffy. She's a toy poodle. But the little devil hates men."

"The dog is a positive non-bitch then," Helen agreed.

"Well, around men she does snap so." Trixie shrugged. "She makes a fuss."

"Fancy that," said Glynis dryly. "If Fluffy goes into a feeding frenzy your date will have his balls torn off."

Gulping for air through a chain of giggles, Helen sputtered, "Bet none of them want to play fetch with Fluffy."

"You two!" Trixie bleated. She removed a photograph showing a thimble-sized, white Fluffy. "She is terribly sweet."

"Look at those fierce black eyes. Eyes black as tires," Glynis joked. "And her fangs go on forever. They could tear the privates off a suitor in absolutely record time."

"Gosh, I'm not showing you two anymore photos. You're just jealous because you haven't got a pet," Trixie charged.

"I wouldn't say that," Helen replied. When she felt Glynis press her fingers beneath her knee, Helen smiled brightly. Those fingers did a tango and she imagined them dancing their way between her thigh and upward. There was an immediate heating. "To say I haven't a pet isn't accurate." She winked across to Glynis. "I've a lovely pet."

Trixie passed the flask to Glynis. "Thanks," Glynis spoke as she poured. "I hope this country isn't bone-dry forever. These stupid little flasks only flavor the tea."

"Oh, you cross girl. I brought a spare," Trixie tittered. "Kiddo, things will eventually change. Of course, in Europe they think Prohibition is Boorish. I explained to them that most of America simply looks away. Like now. The waiter is positively taking every morsel in, but he won't say a word."

"Europe is certainly more liberal, by comparison," Glynis offered. Her hand crawled upward until she felt the heat from Helen's inside legs. "I'm a liberal, by comparison."

Helen cleared her throat. "Trixie tells me that the one negative aspect of being liberal is that many people are too liberal. For instance, in the Alps, she claims, gay men are positively overrunning the place." Her loafer was being slipped off by the nimble shoe of Glynis. She felt a tickle trace her instep.

"They *are*," Trixie reported. Drawing nearer in conference, she divulged, "And women! Lesbians. There are such an awfully lot of them in Amsterdam and Paris. You name it. They seem to have a foothold."

"Foothold?" Glynis rolled her large eyes. "Foothold," she seductively uttered.

"You see them on the streets. In bars. Everywhere. Gertrude Stein is not the only one over there. I've got it on good authority that there is also Colette, Renee Vivien, Virginia Woolf, and there are rumors about Garbo."

"Garbo!" Helen feigned amazement. "Heavenly days!"

"Yes." Trixie crossed her arms. Her head lifted with superiority. "*I* can spot them a mile away."

"However do you manage that, Trixie?" Helen questioned. She felt Glynis give her a warning tap with the cross-strapped, pointed-toe shoe.

"They wear trousers. Almost always they have severe haircuts, and they are very masculine. Some of them have taken to wearing monocles."

"But," quizzed Glynis with a mischievous grin, "if there are also the femme fatale types, then wouldn't they wear feminine garb?"

"Gosh, I'm not sure. But I do have a marvelous way of sorting people out. Mum always tells me I'm insightful," Trixie boasted.

"That's why I'm not frightened to visit Greenwich Village. It's such a hoot." Trixie threw her hands outward. "I go there often. Harlem, too!"

"I imagine you're safe there. Since you are so wonderful at spotting lesbians, I assume you'll easily warn them off." Helen's eyebrows lifted. "I'm amazed that Glynis and I haven't seen you out and about. We also visit the world of sexual hedonism."

"You two have ventured out to places like that?"

"We've ventured *completely* out," Glynis answered with a smirk. "We even have a favorite club in the Village."

"Isn't the jazz an absolute treat?" Trixie asked.

"Of course. But we go for companionship, too." Helen deliberated, and then added, "We go there to be appreciated for who we are."

"Men in the Village also are after me. And you're correct. My money doesn't seem to impress them," Trixie spoke with a smile. "That's so vivifying!" Her eyes anticipated a juicy scandal. "Do either of you actually go out with any of the artist in the Village?"

"We weren't talking about being different because of wealth," Helen explained.

"It would be reckless of us to tell you all the trash at one sitting," Glynis spoke. She then glanced at Helen. Helen nodded affirmatively. "But why not. Helen and I go to a place called *The Creamy Calico*."

"I've heard of that place." Trixie inhaled deeply. "*All* the women are lesbian. Aren't you frightened one of those women might approach you?"

Helen grinned. "We're afraid they won't. That would mean we've lost our touch. But then, we're devoted. Glynis and I have been lovers for nearly two years now."

"Oh, you kid," Trixie roared. She took another gulp of her tea. "You're having a chuckle at my expense, as always. Aren't you?" she asked as her giggles died down. She again swallowed a quick series of sips from her teacup. The silence pressed her. "Well?"

"Glynis has blossom soft skin," Helen divulged with sarcasm.

Trixie glanced from woman to woman. "Golly, I'm sure you're only teasing."

"You stated that lesbians wear trousers. I'm wearing them," Helen remarked.

"Oh, golly! You two aren't even the type. Helen, you're such a stitch." Trixie gave Helen's shoulder a slap.

"Golly, thanks for your vote of confidence," Helen replied. Her back stiffened. "So where would your famous liberal vogue be if you found out we are really lesbians?"

"I *am* liberal," Trixie disputed. "But really! I mean you might go to hell."

"We wouldn't want that," Glynis muttered. "So I guess we'll go *straight* to heaven."

Helen chuckled. "Guess that would make us normal vixens of the Roarin' Twenties."

Glynis licked her lips. "Roarin' rascals just like you, Trixie."

As if on cue, Helen and Glynis reached for Trixie's hands. After sharing a quick smile, the two women frantically scratched their middle fingers inside Trixie's palms."

"Ohhhh…" Trixie uttered as she fainted. Her swooning body limply sagged on the chair.

Helen and Glynis shrugged in chorus. "Gosh!" Helen mocked, "Whatever could be amiss with poor Trix?"

"Pity, just when we were about to explain how to really get to heaven." Glynis clicked her tongue. She dipped a napkin in water and gave Trixie's face a splash.

"Let's call for her chauffer. You and I need to retire to our loft. This has been too very funny. And that makes me romantic," Helen purred.

Both women traded smiles. They watched Trixie blink her way to reality. "Golly, for a minute," she gasped, "I thought you told me that you two are…."

"Women who place our bodies together," Glynis said slowly, sensuously, "and feel the softness that envelops us. We reach orgasmic highs that nearly melt us."

"Kiss deeply enough to reach one another's hearts," Helen added. "We kiss just *everywhere*."

Trixie's eyes widened. "Oh, gosh," she mumbled before passing out again.

"*She's* not what you'd call a proper honey bride," Glynis teased.

"For her it could never be proper," Helen added. "But you, gorgeous, are just proper enough."

One wink later, they stood. After delivering the wobbly-legged Trixie to her awaiting automobile, the two women made their way to a cab.

"Roar for me, baby," Helen requested.

"Meow."

"I'm going to name my pussy after Trixie's birthday gift - Fluffy. And just like Trixie's poodle, my Fluffy doesn't like men either."

Glynis chuckled. "Pets named Fluffy have wonderful taste. Let's go home."

Photograph by Kathie Solie

RULES OF THE BROWNSTONE

Mid 1970s

Papa's Italian rage was boiling over. His fleshy fist hammered on the dinner table. A platter of mounded fettuccini popped right up from the tablecloth. Mama hushed him. Her head nodded toward my sister and me. As if he may not have noticed us watching his rumbling, clattering, and his tantrum. Mama nudged him.

"The girls will hear." To me, she prodded, "Antonia Bernardi, you eat that zucchini salad!"

"Good they hear," Papa continued his tirade. "So they don't go the way of Angie. My oldest daughter is soiled! Sinning with her *girl*friend." Again he hit the table. His face was near to exploding. Another fist rap followed. "Why this family? We never have *this* from my side of the family."

"We'll talk about it later," Mama said, but with a yielding tone. Papa was the decision-maker, and it *was* his tantrum. Mama's soft brown eyes inspected our faces.

Mama realized that my sister, Rosa, was thrilled about our eldest sister, Angie's, trouble. Angie was clearly in deep shit. Rosa, at fourteen, was a scrawny goody-goody. Three years older than me, she was a bookworm and had no boobs whatsoever. Rosa thrived on tattling. And on other people getting their dues. *She* was tickled pink that Papa was having a fit. Angie always joked that his temper was Papa's Italian disorder. Rosa hated anything that Angie had to say. Particularly now that Angie had recently turned sixteen. We knew for a fact that there was magic in that age.

As much as Rosa despised Angie, I worshiped her. I could always be counted on to defend Angie. I told Rosa that Angie didn't have it in her to do anything awful. Last time I jumped to Angie's side, Rosa told me to build my lovely oldest sister a shrine, because I was a brat devotee. Not that I wouldn't have built Angie an entire stadium of shrines, but I didn't have time. I play softball.

When my sneakers drug under the chair, intentionally sounding like a human gas detonation, I giggled. But everyone at the table scowled back at me without even a hint of embarrassing laughter. Nothing but disgust was aimed in my direction.

Whatever Angie had done, it was no minor infraction of the Bernardi house rules. It was major deep shit. Papa hadn't smiled once since sitting down. And Mama was more grim than I'd ever seen her. There was no pre-dinner singing, so it had to have been a very elaborate sin committed by my sister. Mama hadn't even had time to get in a quick novena.

I had the feeling questions were to be answered when Angie arrived. Only *when* that event occurred, Rosa and I were exiled to our room. From that, and the troubled expression on Angie's face, I deduced it would have taken more than a novena, or for that matter, an entire pilgrimage, to make things right.

One advantage of being the youngest is that no one puts a stopwatch on when you go to the bathroom. They've *all* changed your diapers, and probably don't have particularly fond memories of it. So you can stay on the pot the entire day if you like. I slipped into the bathroom and cupped my ear against the crack in the door. I heard it all.

First was Angie's muffled voice. She was not exactly doing back-flips over whatever was wrong. I pressed against the door. Words became more distinguishable. I knew the volume was bound to get stronger. We Italians have a terrific sense of drama in our bloodline.

"It's unnatural!" my Papa shrieked. "My little girls, they got to marry them some good men. Men who will care for and protect their family!" He was hotter than a furnace. I hoped he wouldn't have an attack and go face down in the pasta. His rapid-action temper was in full form. I could imagine his eyes bulging and his face the color of stewed tomatoes. Mama's face was probably the shade of a toasted macaroon. When he goes red, she goes white. "You Mama and me, we want you three to have the best of life. Now who you gonna chose from when the boys find out about this?"

"Papa," Angie resisted, "we don't have lesbian social registries."

"You makin' a joke," he blustered. "Looka your Mama sobbing for you. I work alla these years." Papa was clearly throwing himself on a sword. "Work alla these years. Two jobs I work for my family. And for what? *What?* You gotta *girl*friend!"

Mama interceded. "Maybe she can get help. You know, maybe the priests can do something with her." Mama believed the clergy to be a cure-all.

"Mama," Angie stormed, "I don't want anyone doing anything to change me. It's how I am. I've hidden it away, but I always knew." Her voice sounded tormented, but defiant. "Mama…Papa, I know you're disappointed, but I can't sacrifice my life just to attempt to please you. Ruin my future to keep my past."

"Your life is ruined when you come to your Mama and me and tell us that you sleep with your *girl*friend. Lika man and wife. In sin," Papa wailed. "I rather you go out bonking with the boys than this!"

"It's how I am," Angie insisted, standing her ground.

"An' I tell you how it is. You go from this house," Papa clamored. "We got us rules here. You straighten out or you don't live here no more. You got no family here."

Angie nearly knocked me over when she sprinted past me in the hall. Under her breath she spat, "Male powderpuff mentality!"

Naturally, I tailed her into her room. She flung open her closet. Wildly, she began pitching her clothing on the bed. As soon as she had a huge mountain of clothes, she turned and peered at me. "Well, Toni, are you enjoying the sideshow?"

I sat on the edge of her bed. "How come everyone is yelling more than usual?" I stammered.

"I'm going through my rite of passage." She sat beside me. Her face was filled with distress. "I'm moving over to Tammy's apartment." Her head bowed. "They'll never accept me for how I am."

"How are you?"

"I'm lesbian. I love Tammy."

It took a few seconds for the word *lesbian* to dawn on me. "But how can Italian Catholics be lesbian?"

The first hint of a smile etched on her lips. "It isn't difficult." She then stood. Tossing her clothing into a suitcase, she sighed. "Not difficult at all. But don't worry, hon. I'll be fine."

"Being like that - lesbian, is it a sin? I mean, isn't it against Jesus?"

"Toni, look at it this way. If the creator made us, how can we be wrong? Aren't we designed to follow our hearts?"

"That's supposed to be with men and women."

"Biology teaches that ten percent of most species of animals have same-kind sex." She clamped shut the suitcase. "I don't want to hurt any of you. I love Mama and Papa, but I can't deny my feelings.

Their rules don't fit me."

My arms lassoed her waist. My head crushed against her. "I never heard Papa say it was breaking the rules. Nobody ever mentioned it. Maybe it isn't so terrible after all," I blubbered.

Her hands cupped the back of my head. She squeezed softly; maternally. "Honey, it's forbidden. It's like breaking all the rules at once."

* * *

Observing the sulfur-yellow city sun, I marveled at how complicated it all was. My gaze lowered. I studied the design on my t-shirt. Then I examined the ruffles at the base of my denim cuffs. Twisted, my legs seemed knotted beneath me as I sat outside on the fire escape ledge.

Rosa was in *piss and moan* heaven. For Mama and Papa went from hysterical to hostile. I was left like an eleven-year old hermit. Out on my own.

I worked the out formula just so far. Then my mind blossomed with questions. If

Jesus was really this old time do-gooder, wouldn't he understand about Angie?

After three days, I wondered if answers existed. I was perplexed about this 'rule' business, too. Rules about love and sex are even worse than your basic everyday rules. Naturally, you're not to tell your old misery-pot, Uncle Clarence that his mouthwash isn't holding up. And you can't tell Mrs. Vitelli that the Odor-Eaters she'd placed in her orthopedic shoes years ago have lost all signs of effectiveness. You obey rules to keep from being mean.

But then, Rosa wouldn't break a rule if her life depended on it. And she is a very, *very*, low type when it comes to meanness. So the answer must be that you obey regulations to please your parents.

Angie broke the rules, and she was banished from our house. Aunt Imogene said that young girls living out on their own throw off a scent to horny men. Well, she didn't use the word *horny*, but that was what she meant. *Horny* was my own spin on the interpretation.

Anyway, Papa and Mama never mentioned the details of Angie's leaving. That would have created a commotion. And clearly, Papa and Mama don't want the word out on this lesbian business.

Papa came into my bedroom to say goodnight. I begged him to allow Angie to come home. He wetted down my face with splotched kisses. When I heard a sob catch in his throat, I realized that it was his tears that were making my face damp. His huge, steam-shovel shaped hands then mopped my face.

When he went to the door, he turned off the light. He then paused. He said he loves all three of us. I think he secretly wants Angie home, too.

* * *

I figured that everyone was going to be back to normal by week's end. I fully expected Angie to relent. I expected Mama to talk Papa into allowing lesbianism. But it was a real standoff. No one was giving an inch. They'd all dug in and *in* they were bound and determined to stay. For all times, maybe.

I'd just slapped my textbook shut and dismounted from my desk chair when the phone rang. Mama answered. Her face went paper white. She screamed for Papa. We all gathered. "It's the hospital," Mama relayed. "Angie's been in an auto accident."

Papa's face contorted to anguish. He wept. "I turn my back on my daughter. Now she'sa taken from me forever." He was in a terrible state.

Mama listened intently to the hospital representative. She then replaced the telephone receiver. "Cuts and bruises, but she'll be fine. They'll release her when we get there. We have to sign insurance papers." Mama implored, "Please? She needs us!"

Papa's jaw-band tightened. I figured his temper would be erupting any second. But it didn't even flare. He surveyed Rosa and me. Then he took Mama in his arms. He held her so tightly that I thought he might break her. But she was hugging back. And she was hugging back just as tightly.

Gruffly, he huffed, "We go and get our Angie back now." By the time they reached the door, Papa was back in form. On full blast, he whirled around. "But don't you two think you gonna be lesbians like your sister."

I figured he believes the Bernardi family has its full quota of lesbians.

After we heard the door slam shut, Rosa glared at me. Her eyebrows lifted as she stressed, "*I* wouldn't dream of it."

SWEET AND SOUR

Candy was my thirteen-year old sexologist. She was a year older, and light years beyond me. And to boot, she was a confirmed lesbian. Her mother called her *pudding*. Her father called her *princess*. My folks called her a spoiled brat. They called me by my name, Ophelia. As they had taken so long to figure out a dumb name like that, I guess they weren't about to call me some *precious,* little emblem of a pet name.

Back to Candy. I always liked being around Candy. She gave me pointers that were outrageous.

"Women come in varieties," she lectured.

"Short and tall; light and dark?"

"More than just that. Some have a set of big boomers and some have small ones. Ophelia, I can tell by looking, you are going to be a size A. No matter how you exercise, that's it for you. But let's get on to the really good stuff about women."

"Good stuff?"

"That's right. Listen up. They come in different scents."

Giggling, I leaned back against the edge of her detached garage. We both squatted down, hunkering over our latest discussion on women. My curious nature was zeroing in. "Fragrances? Scents?" I repeated with skepticism in my words.

"Yeah. Don't act like such a ninny. You're still really like a kid," she gruffly insulted me. "This is serious. I'm giving you a treasure trove of information. So listen closely."

I leaned nearer for the lowdown. "Explain scents."

"They smell like either sweet or sour. Naturally, the essences - the bouquet, branches off in subheadings. But basically we're talking sweet and sour."

Laughter detonated through my contorting lips. "I can't help it. I never heard of that." Her glance was broiling me. "I figured you just picked a douche-of-the day flavor and then your aroma was like that. Dripping wildflower or Cherry Supreme."

"You little asshole! If you aren't listening to my words of wisdom, I'll save my wealth of information for someone else. Use it on some other potential dyke. I only selected you because you never miss soccer practice. You do have potential."

"Okay. I'll listen. We were talking scents."

"Yeah. Well, that's what I said. Women are sweet, some of them. Others are sour."

"How many women were in this little test survey?"

"Enough. Just getting a good whiff tells you volumes."

"Come on," I began sputtering again. "How many women have you tipped?"

"Plenty. Plenty! And not only that, they come in different sizes. Down there is different sizes for all women."

"I could have guessed that for myself. Big women are bigger and little women..."

"Naw," she interrupted. "That's got nothing to do with it. One short little thing has a twat that you could drive a dump truck up. And park it beside a Winnebago!"

My snicker exploded into a roar. "So why do you think some women have mammoth ones?"

"Lots of masturbation maybe. Or maybe they took on the entire football squad. Tackles twice. I'm not sure, goofball. I just know some women have whopping big ones," she snitched. "Others could be deflowered by a pinkie." She wiggled her little finger.

When my spurt of giggles continued, she gave me a swat. I straightened up, figuratively speaking. "Okay, so they come in different sizes and smells. What else?"

"When you want a woman, you do this." She opened her mouth and her chunky tongue snaked out and flopped around. Then she tucked it back in. "Well?"

"It looks like you're making kindergarten faces. If you do that a woman might belt you. Or at least call in authorities."

"You are such a pessimistic twerp. I'm trying to give you the benefit of my expertise and you're being a cutesy bitch." She eased her body up along the garage siding. "I'm through wasting my time on you. Forget it. Go out into the world and show how stone ignorant you are. You're probably not an authentic lesbian anyway."

By the time she'd trudged to the end of the alley, I'd muttered, "I wouldn't be too sure of that."

TREASURES

Millennium Y2K

"It's going to be okay," she promised her lover.

Vickie Hampton held tightly to memories of tenderness and affection. Many of those good times were at the kitchen table. Crayons scattered, construction paper was strategically placed, and small handprints completed with finger paints on scrap paper. Designs filled the table. Other memories were of the backyard where balls, sandbox, and an assortment of toys offered a variety of fun.

The modest frame home in suburbia always seemed to have the strum of laughter. There was the propulsion of energy, and just plain fun. It was the house where Popsicles, cupcakes, and juice drinks were dispensed with a smile. Vickie and her lover lived there. And they loved there.

Now, Vickie considered, as she looked across an oak conference table, their family was in jeopardy. They were stationed, solemnly, in an auxiliary courtroom arbitration area.

Vickie's lover, Lisa Porter, had emotionally withdrawn during the last weeks. Vickie understood that Lisa's maternal instinct sensed the danger of their affair. Now, their daughters, Kathy, who had just turned seven, and Becky, nearly four, were being held captive by the courts. Now, Chad Porter, Lisa's ex-husband, was playing legal tug-of-war with Lisa for the children. The daughters were caught in the middle of a custody suit that had been dragging for the past year.

Although Chad remarried, and had been satisfied with every other weekend visits, his mind had been changed. He was no longer cooperative. At first he had encouraged Lisa to find a love of her own. Then two years later it was revealed that Lisa and Vickie were lovers. With that news, he went to court to obtain full custody of his children. His disapproval of his children's *mothers* was evident.

Today, Vickie suspected, there was to be a ruling handed down by an arbitration court. The women had fought valiantly, but it seemed to be in vain. When the accusation is that a parent is lesbian, the women were told by their attorney, the odds are radically changed.

A hush continued. Vickie read the pain in Lisa's bright green eyes. Lisa had conservatively pulled her bronze hair back from her flushed face. A smile faded as quickly as it began. Both Kathy and Becky were carbon copies of their mother. Vickie wondered if the resemblance was part of what endeared her so to the children. It had been an immediate bond. It was as if all parties knew that they each, individually and collectively, loved Lisa.

Vickie touched her lover's hand. "How are you holding up?"

"I'm not certain if I can handle it. If I lose those children, I don't know what I'll do."

"We'll fight until forever," Vickie vowed. The moment the custody battle started, Vickie's own campaign began. She allowed her hair to grow longer in an attempt to look more feminine. Blonde curls now sprayed in an orb around her wide, light face. She wore a skirt, blouse, and pumps. Her days of more radical denims and sweatshirt were a thing of the past. Chad's attorney had called her *gender dysfunctional.* Vickie's appearance now disclaimed that.

"Forever. We don't have forever. Children grow so quickly. Two years ago Kathie was a preschooler. Becky was a toddler."

"I know you've rejected the idea of my having a talk with Chad. But, Lisa, it might help if he gets to know me."

"*I* can't even talk with him anymore. We were married young. If only I hadn't gotten pregnant."

"You wouldn't have given the world those two wonderful little girls."

"I wouldn't be sitting here about to lose them," Lisa said with bitterness.

"Let me plead my case with him. We've tried everything else. I don't see what harm it could do. He's in the next room. I can try to reason with him. Tell him what's in my heart."

"Vickie, our attorney is against it."

"Our attorney makes less money if we settle the dispute. And besides, our attorney isn't getting the job done."

"Chad isn't going to call it off. He's winning."

"Our kids *aren't* winning."

Lisa rustled a stack of papers that were in front of her. "Vickie, I don't want you to talk with him."

"I can be very personable at times."

Lisa smiled. "Let's not complicate this."

"How about if we tell him Kath and Becky were really fathered by a space alien? He has no right to them."

Lisa chuckled momentarily. "There's no way of breaking that news to him gently."

"Please, let me try to talk with him?"

"You really want to talk with him? Take that chance?"

"You told me he isn't a bad person. I know he must have some good qualities. You didn't win him in a raffle, so I assume you loved him when you married him. I want to know him. I've always been better at reading both sides of the situation. I have a right to see if he's a fit person to parent our children."

"What if your plan doesn't work?"

Vickie grinned. "Back to the alien allegation."

* * *

Chad Porter didn't appear to be a bigoted, domineering SOB. With a slim frame, dark eyes, and a short, neatly trimmed, ecru-colored hair, Chad looked like any other businessman. No one denied that he had the welfare of his daughters in mind when bringing the lawsuit to court.

His expression was grim, and nearly embattled. He leaned across the table and glared into Vickie's face. "What's this last minute plea about?" he demanded.

"Chad, you once loved Lisa. I'd venture a guess you still care about her. Just like she will always love what the two of you had. You've shared love. The result of that love is your daughters." Vickie paused a moment. "And your daughters love both of you."

"Look, I don't have anything against you personally. I just don't want my daughters exposed to your lifestyle."

"Chad, it isn't contagious. Statistics show that they're no more likely to be lesbian than any other child. Both Lisa's and my parents were straight. So they won't inherit it, nor will it become some operant behavior by being in our vicinity."

"I just don't want my kids exposed to it. They're getting old enough to understand now." His shoulders stiffened. "It may be familiar ground to you, but I don't want it near my children."

"Children are treasures. Adults are meant to be protectors. I understand you want to protect them. Chad, I've been a parent to them for the past two years. That's the only half of Becky's life she even remembers. The social workers have reported that they're well-adjusted and happy. We've made a kind home for them. It is conducive to their becoming healthy, productive members of society. We love them."

"You *love* their mother."

"They know that we love one another. They see affection, but they don't see graphic sex. They only see the normal things kids see." Vickie took a deep breath. "Chad, under different lighting, we would probably be friends. I admire your fight for them. There's also the fact that you want the best for them. Lisa told me you're a good person. She also said that you and I are very much alike."

"Both assuming the male role?"

"Both of us are decent people. We all care about two little girls." Vickie harnessed her anger. "I'd probably be doing the same thing you're doing. Fighting to make certain they aren't harmed."

"They're young. It won't bother them until they get older. You know how kids are. They'll ridicule them."

Vickie reached across the table. Her outstretched hand tented Chad's fisted knuckles. "Lisa told me you had a difficult childhood. She told me how your parents neglected you. So I understand that you're fighting for them. I can appreciate the fact that you want what's best for them."

"I love kids." He looked down. "I just found out I'm going to be a father again."

"We all love those children. Having more children isn't an option for Lisa and me. But we can all share, and contribute to the upbringing of Kathy and Becky."

"I've always supported the children. I know the actual cost of raising them isn't covered by the child support, but I've always done what I can. I've tried to be reasonable about everything. I've never complained about investing in their lives."

"We've all tried to invest in them. Soccer teams, PTA, camping excursions, music lessons, and everything that goes into making up a family. Chad, I love them, *too*." Her eyes misted.

Fidgeting, Chad glanced away. He pulled his hand from Vickie. Folding them together tightly, he again stared at her. Anger was a pounding force as he talked. "I can give them a normal family life."

"They want their mother. They want to be with us. Chad, right now they're in with their grandmother. Won't you talk with them?

We've done our best to insulate them from the fact that our family might be broken apart. We've only told them that they might be staying with you for a while." Vickie stood. "I'll have them sent in here to be with you. Alone. You tell them that you're taking them away from their mother. You tell them that within a couple of hours they're going to be relocated. You break it to them that the only home they've ever know is going to be taken from them. Tell them that *home* is so fragile it can be disintegrated because of your prejudices and whims. Judge their reaction for yourself. That might give you a clue about what you're trying to do to them."

She reached the door and turned. Her glance was meant to disseminate his expression. But his face was without emotion.

* * *

Lisa moved back from the cove of Vickie's arms. When the door pried open, they looked up with a start. Chad and the children had been in the conference room for nearly an hour. Perhaps he was trying to calm them - or coerce them, Vickie considered.

But when the three walked out, the girls were holding his hands. They seemed unruffled. When they spotted Lisa and Vickie, Kathy rushed to them. Excitedly, she announced, "Daddy says we can stay with him."

Vickie crumbled inside. She felt shockwaves throughout her body. Chad knelt to give his daughters hugs. He stood and addressed Lisa and Vickie. "I told them I didn't think you'd mind if they came to stay with us for a full week this summer. After the baby is born."

Lisa choked her sobs. "You mean you're going to drop the case?"

His head elevated. "They were excited when I told them about their new little brother or sister. But they said they couldn't stay more than a week. Kathy said she couldn't miss practice. Vickie coaches her various sports teams, and she didn't want to let her down. Becky told me she has a new playmate next door." His eyes watered. "They want to belong to us all."

Lisa's walk to him was not rushed. She encircled his neck with her arms. She then sobbed against his chest. Vickie reached down to lift Becky up into her bear hug. With her free arm, she extended her hand. "Thank you, Chad."

He clasped Vickie's arm. "I'd almost forgotten that we promised to spare them pain. Happiness is all I've ever wanted for them."

"And that's exactly what you've given them," Lisa said.

He looked down. "I don't have time to be the soccer coach. Or softball. Or run them to all their lessons. My business is new and it's swamping me. With a new family on the way, well - I just took an accounting." He looked at Vickie. "You spend so many hours with them. Reading to them – sports, and taking them places. I couldn't give them that. To be honest, no matter how much I love them, and would want to, I just couldn't give them the time you give them."

"You give them your love, support, and they know you're there for them," Vickie replied. "That's evident."

With the two girls swinging between their arms, Vickie and Lisa walked the shiny marble corridors out onto the courthouse steps. Lisa instructed, "Girls, wave to your daddy."

Obediently, they flagged their temporary farewells.

"What did you say to him?" Lisa questioned.

"It's what Kathy and Becky said to him that mattered. I just asked him to listen to them. And he did."

Photograph by Kathie Solie

UNSKILLED LABOR

Machinery squealed and barking voices clamored. Equipment noise contended for top billing throughout the one block construction site. A steel girder tethered from the crane above. A fellow construction worker caught Darlene Cooper's attention. "Hey, Coop. We're goin' over to KFC. Want us to bring you a hunk of hen?"

Amused, Coop allowed her wide smile to form a semicircle. She leaned forward, reaching to carefully direct a wobbling beam. "Naw," she replied. "I brought my lunch today."

"Seems like some of the reinforcement beams are missing from the plans."

Coop glanced back across the huge rows of steel. "I saw that. I'll check with Nancy." While her crew secured the beam, Coop considered how difficult it was to discuss anything with Nancy Flynn. It always had been, and especially now.

Coop's tall, athletic figure, short corn-silk-colored hair, low forehead, and large, smoky blue eyes, had been no competition for Nancy Flynn. Coop's ex, Pamela Remington, had fallen for the gorgeous Nancy. Nancy had taken over her father's construction company last year when he retired. So not only was she loaded, Coop acknowledged, but she was also educated, sophisticated, and sexy. Long, jet black hair, mystical grape-green eyes, and an ivory smile intrigued everyone. She even had the polish, personality, and business acumen, to step into her father's footsteps. That had also impressed Pamela.

Coop drove an old pickup. She wore denims, t-shirt, scuffed construction boots, and a hardhat. She lived in a small apartment. There were no flourishes. Pamela had been attracted to Coop's decency, her gentle humor, and her knowledge of the construction world. She also noticed workers at the site had a great respect for her. Bitterly, Coop realized those qualities were not enough to keep the woman she loved. She was no longer a part of Pamela's world. Pamela had *outgrown* the hardworking construction supervisor.

Coop tried to exorcise thoughts of Pamela as she climbed down the scaffold. Any confrontation with Nancy sounded as if Pamela was only a centerpiece – a prize. Coop would refrain from any reference to their private lives. Nancy had always been more interested in the profit line than her father had been when he built the company.

But there were safety guidelines - standards that must meet regulation, and certainly Nancy wouldn't take shortcuts with the plans. Although, Coop recalled, there had been times when corners were cut. Flourishes were skimped on. She had objected, but finally decided that they were nothing serious, just different product lines being substituted. Nancy had never, to Coop's knowledge, shorted plans on potentially dangerous supplies, and products.

Coop felt the air conditioner's breeze when she entered the construction trailer's office. The luxury trailer was moved from site to site in order to accommodate Nancy's penchant for comfort.

Nancy glanced up from her computer. She came around her exquisite cherry wood desk to greet Coop. "Is there a problem?"

"Structural integrity is a problem. OSHA will be on us like a tiger if we short a job."

Nancy went to a small decorative bar, opened the refrigerator and pulled out two cool German beers. She tossed one to Coop. She poured hers in an iced stein. "Have a seat." Coop returned to be seated behind the sentry desk. "Coop, I know we've had our hostilities because of Pamela. But I've kept you on the crew because you're a good worker. Flynn Construction is one of the biggest and best in Nevada."

"What's that got to do with a shortage of trusses? The revised blueprints look as though they've been trimmed. Why?" Coop questioned warily.

"This is the most important project of Pamela's career. She's never been a senior architect on a project of this magnitude. Pam would be terribly offended if she thought unskilled labor doubted her calculation. It would insult her terribly. I know you don't want that."

"Pamela's main concern is that the structure be safe. If we don't have the correct amount of supporting cross beams, it isn't going to bear the load. According to my projections the girders are not substantial and the quantity isn't adequate. They won't support the load."

Nancy interrupted, "Listen to me, lover girl, I don't give a goddamn what your projections are. I've got a structure to erect and a timetable. I've got specifications approved. Your ex-lover, who is my *current* lover, designed those specs. She signed off on the blueprint addendums." Nancy's eyes blazed. "Why don't you go to Pamela and tell her that you're still in love with her, and by the way, she screwed up on the plans. Tell her you have no confidence in her skill as an architect. That ought to go down great." Nancy scoffed, "Pam is bright enough to have left you last year, and she's bright enough to know specs and building materials."

"Let's hope you're bright enough to follow the plans," Coop's drawl stung. She placed the unopened beer back on the edge of the desk. Before she turned to leave, she added, "For everyone's sake, let's hope that. And save the beer. I never imbibe on the job."

"You don't amuse me," Nancy fired. "And you're coming that close to infuriating me," she said while holding up her thumb and index finger.

Coop's jaw band tightened. She slammed the door shut. Ambling back to the scaffold, she considered Nancy's accusation. Coop was still in love with Pamela. She capped her head with the hardhat and began her ascent.

For the same reasons she loved mountain climbing, she loved working on high beams. Coop was excited when seeing the great horizon from the height advantage atop the skeletal building. There was also an edge of danger. She conceded there was something to the theory that danger was a powerful aphrodisiac. However, even a brilliant climb hadn't *charged* Coop the way Pamela Remington had. Each time she neared Pamela, her heart raced. Even after they'd been together five years. That was nearly one-sixth of her thirty-one years. They'd shared half a decade together, and Coop had planned to share a lifetime.

Coop had been working for Flynn Construction for over two years when she took Pamela to an office party. Nancy moved in on the novice architect with determination. The Flynns *were* the construction industry in the state. They were well-connected. Nancy's promises to the ambitious young architect made her seem more than a benevolent mentor. Within a week the most prestigious construction firm in the state had hired Pamela as Flynn's in-house architect.

From there Nancy's attention continued to be on Pamela. There were luncheons, flowers, and finally an evening dinner meetings. Pamela was won over, and impressed by the sophisticated construction company owner.

Coop wasn't certain why she'd decided to stay on at Flynn. Perhaps, she declared to herself, it was to be near Pamela. To catch a glimpse of her ex-lover as she made her way to the executive trailer each morning. Coop felt her heart turn stone-hard with that confession. She scanned the partially built structure. Her eyelids blinked with the sun. She took her sunglasses from her breast pocket and put them on.

Suddenly, she heard the clatter of falling steel. There was a strain, the groan of several beams before they snapped. Coop twisted around to see the crashing beams as the concrete reinforcement wall crumbled. As if the structure had been detonated, it trembled before collapsing on the scaffolding beneath.

Coop experienced an immediate twist in her stomach. She sprinted to the rubble. Three crew members had been crushed. The project's worst scenario had released terrifying pandemonium. Disaster was the name of the scene.

* * *

Pamela Remington's new Mercedes skidded around the corner. She'd received word of the tragedy while on her way to the site. When her cellphone rang, she thought it might be Nancy asking why she was late for their luncheon tryst. They'd planned a relaxing catered lunch in Nancy's trailer. But Pamela's lover delivered the message of an accident with a faltering voice.

Now, Pamela cursed under her breath as she pulled her sleek vehicle inside the fenced site. Ambulances were leaving. Police and building investigators remained.

She entered the office. "Nancy?"

Nancy bolted to the door. She grasped her lover. Pamela's streaked sepia-colored hair was pulled back behind her neck and held with a bright blue scarf. It matched her stylish suit. Her brown eyes dimmed. Her alabaster smile had faded. She had only glanced toward the cordoned area where the tragedy occurred. Officials were milling around the jumbled, littered site.

Nancy took Pamela in her arms. "Babe, two are critical and were transported to the hospital. The third man died."

With disbelief, Pamela shook her head. "How could this have happened?"

"Pammy, you're going to find out about this. Investigators are out there now. I had to make certain adjustments."

"You mean you altered the plans? Changed specifications?"

"I rearranged the blueprints with fewer joists."

Incredulously, Pam asked, "You shorted materials?"

Pensively, Nancy lifted her lover's jaw and kissed Pamela passionately. When Pamela buried her head against Nancy's shoulder, Nancy pleaded, "You've got to help me. You can put an addendum in. You could smuggle it into your office files. I'd have a duplicate. It could work."

"You want me to lie?" Pamela moved away. She glanced over at the blueprint canisters on the desk. "Everything has been filed. A phony addendum is too dangerous."

"Pammy, listen to me. We're in this together. Consider the professional liabilities. You'll probably only be reprimanded. You're young - this is your first major project. They'll forgive you. I'll go to bat for you. They'll believe it was only a miscalculation by a fairly inexperience architect. Nothing more. There won't even be charges. It's an innocent error."

"A man is dead. Two are critical. That's no innocent error."

"Flipside is damned grim. The worst case scenario is that they'll indict me for skimping on materials. Honestly, Pam, I never thought it would matter. But legal charges could wipe out the company. No one would touch us. Flynn Construction pays for our luxurious home, the plane, cars, our vacations, jewelry, clothing - everything."

Pamela closed her eyes. "But my reputation is on the line, too."

"Please, Pam, this is even more serious. I could be sentenced on a manslaughter charge. Not only would we lose everything, I would lose you if I were to be incarcerated." Nancy's eyes begged. "I've given you everything I could. I've been there for you. I gave you this job in the first place." She embraced Pamela. Whispering into her ear, she begged, "Please, babe. Please. Just do this for me. You won't regret it. I love you."

"Nancy, this is a criminal act."

"Pam, please. I know you've talked about marriage. I'll marry you. Anything you ask."

Pamela felt the same chills she felt when Nancy first held her. She was again overwhelmed by Nancy's touch. She clutched her lover tightly. When their embrace ended, Nancy traced the lips of her lover with her own. "I love you, too," was all Pamela could say. She then asked, "What about the media?"

"I've had all the calls switched back to the office. I told my staff there to stall."

There was urgency in her voice. "Please, Pamela. Don't let me down. Babe," Nancy implored. Her arms wreathed Pamela, "Please say you'll help me. I couldn't stand prison. And mostly, I couldn't stand being without you."

"I'll do as you ask." Pamela surrendered. She wasn't certain if she could stand not having Nancy in her life. "Nancy, why? Why did you short the specs?"

"Monetary concerns. Babe, costs were escalating. I didn't mean for this to happen. You know that."

Pamela wished she felt Nancy's betrayal without her own guilt. She'd searched her emotions constantly since becoming Nancy's lover. She never quite knew where this love expedition was going to go. Perhaps, she reflected, the mystery was part of the allure. She considered her own culpability. Suddenly she realized she was thinking of Coop's stern warning. She had told Pamela that Nancy was unethical.

Although she never knew where the adventuresome Nancy might take her, she always knew where Coop would take her.

* * *

"You'll end up twisting in the wind. She'll get away with it," Coop grumbled. She leaned back against the shiny midnight-blue Mercedes. She hoped Pamela wouldn't start the ignition before she'd be allowed to have her say. "Pamela, why are you taking the fall?"

"I'm in love with her. Maybe it's loyalty."

"Don't flipping talk to me about *loyalty*," Coop snapped. When she saw Pamela fish her purse for keys, Coop apologized. "I'm sorry, Pam. Please just talk with me a minute. Explain to me. Why are you willing to take her hit?"

"I've explained as much as I know." Pamela looked up at the sun. Her squint was one of pure pain. "Coop, I'm sorry that you don't accept Nancy and I are together. Being together means protecting one another. It wasn't as if Nancy wanted this to happen."

"She isn't protecting you," Coop replied sarcastically. "You're the one taking the blame." Without hesitation, Coop added, "The woman has smutty values. But I always believed you had integrity."

"I need to deal with all this, please don't start. Coop, just please back away."

"Back away! Nancy's profit margin killed a man. And injured two others. Men with families. They trusted her. They trusted you. And the worst part about it for me is that they trusted me."

Pamela reached. Her fingers drifted over Coop's fist. "I feel badly enough. Don't do this to me."

"Pam, it can be put right. Tell the truth."

"I'm trying to be there for her."

"She's breached the trust of her employees. If she gets away with this, who can tell when it will happen again? And have you considered what might have happened if the building came down with hundreds of innocent people inside? Pamela, she committed a crime. I warned her over and over. Even today I stormed her office and confronted her. I saw what happened, so maybe I'm to blame. But I thought together *we* could convince her. She cut corners to buy all the things that impress you. All the things I could never have given you."

"You're turning your anger on her. But face it, you'll never get over the fact that she took me away from you."

"That may be part of it. But my anger goes beyond that. You're victimized by it all," Coop alleged. "You trusted her, too. Now you're defending her."

"Be honest. You hate her because of me."

"I still have feelings for you," Coop admitted.

"It's too late for us, Coop."

"Do you know for certain that it's too late? Can you tell me that all your feelings for me are gone?"

"Coop, I only care about you as a friend. Nothing more." Pamela turned the ignition key. "The way you feel about me, I feel about her. Now, can you understand?"

Coop's vocal cords felt knotted. Her heart ached. She watched the Mercedes sway toward the street. Silently, she allowed pain its moment.

* * *

"Babe," Nancy boasted, "I'll take care of you. Don't worry. We've got the best representation money can buy. Our bases are covered." Nancy rolled her office desk chair back. "The project is back on schedule. Blueprints were switched out. We're covered."

"Your ass is covered. That's what you mean."

You must have been talking with that dyke ex of yours. Coop

was giving you the wit and wisdom of unskilled labor. She even filed a report, but I told the officials that she was a trouble-making malcontent. Pam you'll see, this is for the best."

"My career is not only on hold, it might well be over," Pamela predicted. "Are you concerned that I'm taking the blame for it all?"

"Of course I'm concerned," Nancy answered. She came from behind the desk. "I'm suffering for both of us. I just meant that this is the only way we can stay together."

"If I recant my testimony, now, I can save what shred of reputation I have left."

"There's no reason for that. Even if you recant, you've become an accomplice. Right now, we've got an accident. If you talk, we've got a crime." Nancy clasped her lover to her. "Don't worry, we're a team. You can stay on here at Flynn, or I'll give you the startup money to begin your own firm."

"Don't worry. I'm not going to tell anyone." Pamela moved from her lover's arms. She looked out the window. She saw Coop suspended on a beam. "It could have been Coop beneath the rubble."

"But it wasn't. She's fine. She's so fine that this morning she not only unloaded on me again, but she gave me her two-week's notice."

"And your business is fine again. She's always been a thorn in your side. She tried to warn you." Pamela's face was covered in distain. "She knew something like this would eventually happen."

"She was always moaning about something or other. Babe, I made an error in judgment. If it wouldn't have been for third quarter deficits, I wouldn't have revised your plans. I wasn't thinking."

"Don't blame this on the foibles of being human. Or the cost over-rides. Don't do that." Pamela walked slowly to the door. She turned, "I've got thinking to do."

"Come on, you know you're in love with me. It's too late to turn back."

"Funny, that's what I told Coop." Pamela glanced back at Nancy's scowl. "I won't breathe a word. Your secret is safe. But keep one thing in mind. Sometimes we just think it's too late. I'm leaving you, Nancy. And if you ever mess with the specs again, on any project, I'll find out. And I'll blow whistles until your ears fall off. Do you understand that?" she asked through her teeth.

"You're walking out on me?" Nancy asked with amazement.

"Yes. And I'm warning you. Don't ever do anything that can harm anyone." She inspected Nancy's bewildered face. "I'll pick up my things when I've found an apartment."

"You're not going back to Coop?"

"She's probably too smart to want me back." Pamela tightly slammed the door. She went to her car for her hardhat. She walked to the scaffolds.

"What you doing out here?" Coop questioned as she gazed down at Pamela.

"Can you come down a minute?"

Coop lowered her trim body. She moved with care, but with the acrobatic skill of a child on a jungle-gym set. She stood with hands on hips, her hat dipped forward. "Yes?"

"You've resigned from Flynn Construction?"

"Yep."

"Me, too. Actually I'm leaving Nancy. You were right. In my heart I tried to exonerate her. I can't." There was a long, dead silence. "Coop, I know I said it was too late for us."

"And I finally believed you." She groped for words. "Pam, I can't love you again. The respect is gone. The love is gone. I couldn't love you the way you loved her. You love her enough to be unethical. You became unethical for her. I could never love anyone that much. I wouldn't want to." Coop watched Pamela blinking away tears. "I guess it's a good thing that I finally stopped believing my dreams, and finally started believing your words."

Coop's fingers tightened around the steel bar. She began her ascent. *Too late,* she mused. Love doesn't run by a time clock. It runs by a heart. And her love for Pamela had ticked down to emptiness.

WINTER WINE

1993

Faint tension lines appeared to be tattooed on Roxanne Marsh's face. Those lines might have been produced by her early morning flight from New York to San Francisco. But it was far more complicated than that. For her flight had only allotted time for Roxanne to confront her sorrow. After a hasty cab ride to the hospital, she realized how near she was to Ted.

Once there, in a small, drab waiting room, she'd flipped through several magazines. But she saw pages that dredged up memories. She attempted to interpret those bittersweet remembrances. She wondered why guilt invaded each time she thought of seeing Ted Cameron. Perhaps, she feared, she might not be able to conceal the revulsion. His sickness and his dying was not only an epidemic, it was an epidemic fueled with fear.

Her emotions had never been cloistered from Ted's unique insight. They certainly wouldn't be now. She confronted her prejudice. It was buried, but not deeply enough to go unnoticed.

With a toss of her stylish, neck length, sable hair, she glanced away from the people walking through the hospital's bleak corridor of the hospice wing. Her lips were solacing. Their usual gregarious pout was absent. Her lissome body tensed. There was only paleness on her usually rose-colored face. And there was no sparkle in her golden hazel eyes. Not now.

She fidgeted while a man called Gordon something-or-other introduced himself as Ted's friend.

"Ted's spoke of you often. He calls you *Marsh-mellow* sometimes. I didn't know what the hell you were," Gordon joked. His humor was meant to be outrageous. "I thought maybe you were a drag queen."

"Now you know. And I'm certainly not a drag queen," she added her disclaimer with disgust.

"Did you know before this that Ted rides sidesaddle?" Gordon broke into her thoughts with his whooping cackle.

"Of course I knew. We've been friends for years," she answered with tentative angst. "When *I* was coming out, Ted was the first to know. He even helped me understand."

"I've gotten close to Ted in the last few weeks. I'm his deathwatch buddy." With a morbid, churlish laugh, Gordon added, "I conduct the AIDS cemetery shuttle. We go hospice to heaven, or whatever destination."

Roxanne's disapproval of his statement wasn't veiled. Nor was the fact that she disliked his effeminate, stiffly wooden gait. No portion of his homosexuality was obscured from view.

Gordon sighed dramatically. "You don't look like a lesbie, dear," he finally said. He shifted in his chair.

Initially Roxanne thought about lashing back. She could tell the mid-forty aged belle that he certainly would never be mistaken for straight. She wouldn't. Although Gordon was obviously ill, his flouncy mannerisms showed energy. Roxanne wasn't sure why Gordon's continuous babble about the *girls* bothered her so. Perhaps she felt the same way about mannish women. With that admission, she felt uncontrollable guilt. She knew her bias shouldn't be, but was.

She finally spoke. "Gordon, I hope my appearance makes me look like what I am. A woman. And yes, I am a lesbian. My appearance is my identifiable gender wrap."

"My, *my,* but we are touchy," his simulated falsetto blurted.

"My friend is dying."

"Well, you came just in time. You've dropped by to sit in the mourner's cheap seats. Attending an afternoon decomposition of an old friend isn't easy." Gray stubble haloed his small head. Purple snail-like eyes were distended from charcoaled eye sockets. He blinked his heavily-veined eyelids with drama as he crossed his legs. "What's your motive for joining the deathwatch?"

"I love Ted." Wearily Roxanne closed her eyes. Following a prayer-like pause, she disclosed, "I'm not thrilled about your calling this visit a deathwatch."

"Whew! Parental discretion is advised." Gordon's comment stung as badly as an acid burn.

Roxanne's grimace was automatic. A combative tangling of emotions roared through her. She considered Gordon and his ilk offensive. "I would have made the trip sooner, but I wasn't aware of his condition until a couple days ago."

"When the death warrant is served; it is served."

Roxanne always thought of death as a cruel joke. Gordon's

vocalizing with grim gallows humor only confirmed it. If there were a creator, the practical joke being perpetrated on Ted was more than she could stand.

Ted. Roxanne momentarily rested her eyes when their lids lowered. She hated facing Ted. His robust handsomeness was imprinted on her mind. Agile, athletic, and proud, Ted and been her *date* through college and beyond. The ruse was convenient for both of them. They didn't need to skirt the quiz of nosy friends, family, and employers. Men backed away when she lovingly placed Ted's photograph on her desk. Everyone accepted their relationship. Then a few years ago, she moved to the East Coast, and it became a long-distance romance. The world bought into her *romance* story. After all, they spoke once or twice a week, and commuted back and forth half a dozen times a year.

So now, how could this bright, sensitive, witty young man become prematurely devoured by a ravaging virus? She spoke her question out loud. "How can this be happening to Ted? He's only thirty-two. I can't get my mind around it. He's one of the world's most gifted film editors and he's dying of AIDS. I think the term is – fallen in his prime. He's only a year older than I am," she murmured helplessly. "Needless. His dying is needless."

"It wasn't the sex that got him. It was the additive, dear," Gordon answered with a snicker. "Well, anyway, he'll be glad you made this bereavement junket. Not a thrilling trip for you." His voice dueled with her conscience. "Am I correct, dear?" His sharp, pointy teeth seemed to spring from an intuitive smile.

"I'll hate seeing him like this. That goes without question," she conceded. "We like to secure our memories with happy thoughts. Not a final image of him wasted away, emaciated." Mired in a moment of self-actualization, her eyes were curtained shut with a blink. When they flashed open, an inner-dispute was evident. She'd often been teased by lovers that her luminous eyes were tattletales. Her eyes became *tattling topaz of the night*, one lover poetically had expressed to her.

"When did Ted tell you?" Gordon's semi-snarl probed.

"When I saw him last time I was here, four months ago, he looked thin. He told me he was dieting. I had suspicions. Then a couple of months ago he had been doing a TV project in New York. We planned a luncheon. When we met, I knew. I knew he was sick." Roxanne glanced away, remembering the words he used. Although she recognized that he looked so haggard. "He claimed he kept it from me so I wouldn't worry."

"Ted's a class guy. On the other hand, I just phoned everyone I knew and told them I'd finally picked up a case of prick flu."

Roxanne inhaled the soapy disinfectant odor of the hospice wing of the hospital. Her eyes lifted as her voice trembled. "He's always been the strong one in our relationship. He's the one who came to my rescue. Broken affairs, career decisions, whatever - he was there. He even got me in with the network where I work. His spiel moved me up the executive ladder. At least that's what I believe. None of it could have been possible without his help. I owe him so much."

"Sister and brother success story! My, my. Many *dykes* hate all men. Gays included," he assaulted.

"I don't appreciate that derogatory appellation."

Gordon's eyes registered. He'd hit this woman's hot button. "Maybe you aren't a dyke. But darling, I am a rump ranger. A fudge packer. I'm a *faggot*. All the ugly words they pitch at us – I am. Since I'm on my death journey, if I can't be okay about sticks and stones now, when can I be? Where can I be safe, if not in my two-room, slum apartment?" His eyes snapped. "I was a decorator. I lived in a wondrous Victorian mansion. Restored by me, naturally. Garden all done up, lots of flowers. Pansies, too. I can relate to successes, dear. But this dying business is an expensive event. The admission price is not really worth it. We pay by the month, rather than by the year. Oh, well, the admission fee allows me to show the world my heart. Without fear. I'm fine with wearing the fag badge if I want. You, my dear, can't even say the word *dyke*. That is a well-hidden lez."

Roxanne was relieved when the nurse entered. She handed her a gown and rubber gloves. She asked, "Is this necessary?"

"Yes," the nurse insisted. "It's more for your friend's protection than yours."

Chaffing, Gordon snickered. "Another germ or two isn't going to make him a goner one bit faster." When the nurse glared, he shrugged. "Frankly, in a few days his fight will be over. My death sentence doesn't put me far behind."

As the nurse left, Roxanne felt the urge to follow behind her. To escape. "Gordon," she said mechanically, "I'm sorry you've been stricken with this horrible virus. With all my heart, I wish AIDS had never been inflicted on the world."

Gordon coughed. "The lord's little faggot roundup. I've been a buddy for so many. After my lover died, I took up the cause. When he was dying there was a song on the radio about love making the world go around. On his deathbed, he smiles up at me. Tells me that love can make our world go *off*. Profound, don't you think? He was a biochemist."

"Ted's lover is gone, too."

"We keep offering up. Appeasing angry gods, I wouldn't wonder."

"Or goddesses." Roxanne's words were not combative. Only speculative.

Gordon giggled. "I've never consider that. Maybe a female deity did screw us over."

Roxanne looked away. "Maybe it's the horrendous luck of the draw." She examined the sign hanging on the wall behind Gordon. ISOLATION WARD, it read. Penciled beneath were the words someone erased. Impressions were yet visible. QUEEN'S ROW. Then below that DEATH ROW was scrawled. Vehemence accompanied her sadness. With hopeless hostility, she lamented, "Ted has never harmed anyone in his life. Why would a supreme being have it in for Ted?"

"My theory is that it's a tutti-fruiti offering on a sacrificial altar. We daisy-chainers designed the pearly gates, so we can't wait to see them." His laugh diminished into a hoarse cough. "God has an open season on fags. The net is coming down. We're dying out by natural selection."

"I understand your anger." Roxanne thought about how devastating it would be if she were to lose her lover at such a young age. No one expects to lose lovers and best friends all before reaching forty.

"Understand? You're in a low risk category, dear. You really can't be expected to understand last gulp gulch. This is our penalty for loving. We're sacrificed to a gaming god. Random selection may not come in. No. Hell, no. The queens are being polished off."

"Ted is not a queen," she quickly disputed.

"No matter." Gordon's face went bisque pale as he sucked for the next breath. "Countdown. Regardless of how we fall on the masculinity chart. We're names on a cure waiting to be found. And it's too flipping late for Ted. And me. He wasn't a slut, you know?" Gordon defended.

"I know that."

"He had an affair with an infected actor. The guy did a lot of sleeping around before meeting Ted. I, however, was an all-out whore. Doesn't matter. Soon we are all to be gift-wrapped by a mortician. Up we go to Saint Peter. Maybe the name Peter is the attraction. Saint Peter." Gordon's laugh was vicious. "What a crock. Saint Peter dressed up in a Captain Marvel outfit. But he's been made up by a drag queen. Spare no mascara. We appease the gods. We're being exterminated. Our little death ministry. Until enough *normal heterosexuals* fall, we're on our own."

"I agree. It isn't fair." She was angry. This helplessness was an extra-strength variety. It stirred previously vacant places in her soul.

"If the disease," he bitterly impeached, "had started centuries ago, we'd have been missed. Baudelaire. Tchaikovsky, Wilde, Gide, Plato, Proust, Whitman, Leonardo, Michelangelo. For their proclivities, their art would have die with them. All the lewd pansies would have gone to the viral firing squad at one time. Like now."

"Some straights do understand, but not all," she admitted glumly.

"Ah, well, we've been good for the coffin business," he clamored with a braying laugh.

"Business," she repeated. "Does Ted have the funds for hospitalization and final expenses? I have savings."

"He's fine. Unluckily, Ted won't outlast his bucks. He asked that the remainder of his account go for a party. No service. Just a party. A couple of minutes to play the old John Lennon song, *Imagine*, and that's it. Simple enough. I'll call and let you know the details. Ted enjoyed underplaying everything. I want a fucking twenty-one canon salute and add in an orchestra parading down a main street. Not Ted. He wants a song, and then farewell."

"Ted has always hated extravagance," Roxanne agreed with a mellow smile. "Yes. That's what made him a brilliant film editor." Wistfully, she recalled, "He wanted to be a director until he edited his first movie. Then he rearranged his aspirations. He told me that a director makes a film. An editor makes love to a film."

* * *

When the nurse beckoned, a wide brush stroke of loneliness covered Roxanne Marsh. Walking toward Ted's room was beyond any anguish she'd ever known. Awkwardly, she reached to untie the flapping mask that the nurse had hurriedly looped. She studied the umbra shadows that followed through the dim hallway. Reality told her that it was her own willowy frame casting those images. But they were not to be touched or caught.

Her walk skidded when she reached Ted's room. An icy, twisting truth stabbed at her. She didn't want to see him like this. Her heart hammered. Her throat strained. She wasn't obligated, she argued. But she was directly above a trapdoor. He knew she was there.

She entered the tiny crypt of a room.

Their gaze corded. She studied his skeletal form. Ted's sunken face began to contort. He expelled a rattling cough. Motioning for her, his hand moved with palsied effort. His face was ravaged. His blanched skin, with the translucency of raw egg whites, was dotted with liverish blotches.

She recalled his once handsome face. Dark expressive eyes, with awning brows had become shrunken mahogany shades. Seclusion ended when those eyes glinted with recognition. They prowled one another's face. Anemic pallor, the grizzled look of death, covered him. Palmate hollows exaggerated gruesome splotches on his forehead and cheeks. His once muscular shoulders had melted into pasty knobs beneath his hospital gown.

"Rox," his voice trembled. "You look close-up terrific. Rumor has it you're going to be the next network president."

"Even as we speak, a takeover is in the works," she joked. Reaching, she touched his face. Realizing she wore rubber gloves, she snapped them off in two fierce, explosive yanks. Both hand cupped his bony face. "Ted, I'd have come earlier. I had no idea how quickly...." Her lips moved as words formed, but stalled - stillborn.

"I kept it from you on purpose. When we talked, I always made up something I was doing so you wouldn't come. I know you wanted to. I wanted you to remember our best days. We had a wonderful background. It's been a complete friendship. We always accepted one another." His mica eyes dulled. "Glad to see you for a final time. I know this can't be easy for you."

Their fingers laced, just as they had so many times before. She tucked his hand into hers, trying to take care not to move the IV needle. Protectively, redemptive, she gave a tender squeeze. His papier-mâché grasp went limp. Tinsel-thin vessels wound beneath his drawn skin. He was alive, she thought. But in days would not be.

"I met your buddy, Gordon."

"He's a tart," Ted acknowledged with a slight grin. "Hell, Marsh, he makes me laugh with his outrageous thoughts. Claims the world will be a far less bitchy place without him. He says he hasn't found a soul that disagrees with that."

Ted's profile was wren-like. Roxanne wanted to restore him to health. She didn't have the power. Her eyelids veiled with a prolonged blink. "Ted, I can't even begin to image what you're going through."

"I've got my feet firmly planted on ice and a layer of nothingness," he kidded. His guttural words tapped with each shallow breath. "Never could ice skate."

"No. Another of our commonalities. Ted, I don't want to lose you."

Only slightly above a whisper, he spoke, "Death is an uncharted area." With a natural stoicism, as if empting out his soul, he stated, "I haven't heard a supreme being's voice-over yet. There's a curiosity about my next frame. Gordon says we're being rocked by a death cradle. The alarm is going off. Completion," his weak voice faded. "At first I thought it was a dream. I expected to awaken. It would be like some yesteryear film outtake tossed on a cutting-room floor. I thought someone would pick me back up and keep me in the movie."

"You don't deserve this," she faintly responded.

"None of us do. We didn't decide on a mass suicide plot to satiate the Religious Right. To make amends for our sexual orientation by the ultimate sacrifice." Gloomily, he offered, "Death is being tired. As it approaches, my soul is being pressed away. Damn it, Rox, I hate being a statistic." The corners of his mouth trembled. He disclosed, "A few years ago I was banned from the family portrait. Now, it's the family plot. I'll be planted in California."

"We did our best to give our respective families what they wanted. For so many years they believed we were lover. We were *acceptable*. So much time was stolen by lies. There were times we needed to pretend for their benefit. And in the end, nothing was enough."

"Is your family still snubbing you?"

"Still. And you're closer to me than my own brothers. Now, I'm losing you. It makes me so angry."

"Don't be angry. I've tried. It doesn't cure AIDS."

Roxanne returned his smile. Then a drizzle of tears spurted from her eyes. Warmth scalded as the wetness streamed. "I wish I knew how to handle this better."

"You'll be fine."

"Ted, you mean so much to me. I wish you knew how much I'll

miss you."

"I'll miss the human race. We're all on a ship. Our end of the ship is sinking."

Cordoned from the moment, she felt the lifeboat capsizing. "I love you."

"I love you, too." When the nurse entered, he groaned. "Timing. I was just telling my best lady that I love her," he bantered.

"You're more coherent today than you've been all week," the nurse commented. "Mr. Cameron, do you like pretty women now?" She chuckled as she injected a syringe into the tubing coupler. "A little something to help you sleep. You'll be getting drowsy soon."

In a mock secret, he whispered to Roxanne, "She mixes a staunch morphine cocktail."

Roxanne scanned the room. Watching tessellating blinks of light as the window blinds quivered, she attempted to trace her memory. The day Ted won the state championship trophy at a track and field meet. He'd winked in her direction. The day had been clear and fresh. She wondered if the strong aroma from earth clods that surrounded nearby plants had triggered that recollection. Muskiness mingled with scents of disinfectant. No matter what brought on the memory, it was treasured.

When the nurse left the room, Roxanne asked, "Remember wining State?"

"My heart was a giant fist when I crossed the tape."

"No one has ever broken your record."

As they reminisced Roxanne witnessed the years flowing past like great rivers. They were all to return to the same lake. Their past. Time insisted on abridging their conversation. Instinctively, they realized their friendship didn't need to be reinvented. It was braided – it was bonded forever.

A silence glutted the moment. Even silence fastened them. The ticking of his breath seemed perilous. When the drapes of his eyes began to droop, Roxanne realized for the first time, truly, that he was leaving her.

He requested, "Two things, Marsh. Stay well, and stay with me until I drift off to sleep."

"I'm right here."

"We have awesome memories." His flash of a smile waned. "Those days were like fine wine. Wine usually improves with age. But sometimes it sours before used."

She clamped her eyes tightly shut. She turned her face. Her

hands reached up, and she wept into them. How many nights the two of them had shared a bottle of fine wine. They'd shared laughter and shared friendship.

"Maybe there's something better out there," she forged optimism.

"Rox, remember the time I fell at the track meet. I told you that my injury wasn't as bad as it looked."

"You're knee was pulp."

With a kindred grin, he confessed, "It felt like pulp."

"You clung to your macho image," she challenged.

"Yes. But it was a son-of-a-bitch. I nearly chewed the inside of my lips off. I'd told you it wasn't the worst thing in the world." Blinking back tears, he added, "I was right. It wasn't. *This* is the worst thing. This is it, Rox."

"Maybe there's more."

"Death also might just be a frame dissolving to empty."

With an excruciating nod, Roxanne conceded, "Perhaps. Ted, why don't I stay? I have enough vacation time. I can be with you."

"No," he firmly answered. Their eyes locked. With a braced courage, a chivalry, he repeated, "No. Of all the people I don't want here, it's you."

"Me?"

I want you to remember our sunshine. And," with an indulgent, big brother tone, he pronounced, "I want you to remember we're all family. Brothers and sisters. You tend to forget that."

"I know. We're different shades of the rainbow. And I do forget. Sometimes I want to shout that I'm Sapphic. Other times I just want to hide. Hide," she repeated with a grin of embarrassment. "I'm on Gordon's side of the ship, right?"

"Right, Marsh. It's more important than ever. We've got to remember that now. Queens and diesel dykes might be the battering rams announcing our existence. But it takes everyone to make our statement. We need solidarity. Whatever *any* of us might be, all of us are. No one of us is the enemy. They're us. We're them."

His shallow breathe eased. Their final glance fused. His heavy lids fell. Watching as he slept, she tried to synchronize their breathing. She wanted to inhale for him. She could not. For the next hour she sat beside him. A hush, unlike any other, invaded her heart.

She meditated. It seemed one of life's most atrocious pranks. Trawling for a miracle only intensified her pain. Roxanne had never

marched in an activist's parade before. She'd never declare herself.
She vowed to do both.

And then, as his sleep deepened. She kissed his forehead, and
then left his side.

* * *

Roxanne sat opposite Gordon in the waiting room cubical. She
tore off the paper gown.

"Good of you to come down among the lepers," Gordon said
with a scowl. The cool gleam of his almond-shaped eyes jabbed.
We're all just strange petuties from the daisy review. Wilting away, a
petal at a time." His glance suddenly scorched with hatred. "We're
queuing up for our turn in that final fuck." Looking up as the hive-
conversation of whispers came from the nurse's station, he revealed,
"Bets. They're placing bets on tonight's death toll. No celestial
Hegira included in this little tragedy, dear. We're driving the census-
takers wacky. We don't even make good eunuchs when we're ill.
Think we'll become extinct?"

"Gordon," Roxanne protested, "I haven't done anything to you.
Why are you upset with me?"

"I'm next in line to die." His melancholy was restrained. "I view
death in the extreme. My dreams are of a Nordic hunter chasing me
with a scythe. He hacks away at me from the moment I fall asleep.
Every night, his blade swings at my gashed body. Until morning.
Then I realize I am on the guillotine scaffolding. It wasn't a
nightmare."

"Death is never fair."

"Once I thought life is just the beginning of immortality. I
went through Nam believing I was destined to live throughout
eternity. I told myself a lie in order that I might live. Now, our most
tragic truth is that we've contaminated one another."

"Gordon, no one knew."

He stood, strutted to the door. He turned and fired, "No use in
being depressed, dear. What a delight life is." His perverse chuckle
broke into a sprinting laugh. His face contorted to a gasp. Tears began
to tumble from his eyes. Uncontrollably, his voice wrenched. "I wish
someone loved me."

Roxanne moved to his side. Her arms extended. She held him,
grasping him tightly to her. What had started as his joke became
authenticity. She released him from her clasp long enough for them to

view one another's suffering.

"Ted told me to love you," she explained.

"Me?" he questioned between sobs. "I thought you just loved Ted."

Her jaw line was taut with tenacity. "That's what I thought, too. But I was wrong. I was an outsider. Now I'm going to belong to my true family."

With these words Roxanne realized she was no longer trapped in summer. But she wondered why autumn had vanished before she'd come to know it.

Kieran York

WORDS FROM A SPINNING STAR

"You say not to move?" he questioned.

"Please hold that pose for me a moment longer," she answered.

"Ain't no pose. I'm just not doin' anything."

Long ago dismantled, the derelict was a scarecrow without mission. For certainly, despair exuded. That quality was easily captured by the camera lens. Jed Ellison's time-battered face filled up the frame of Marlane Hunter's viewfinder. Zooming to immortalize that desolation, she focused her camera with the same confident aplomb that made her an award-winning photographer.

Each image shot on that camera was sacred.

Her beloved mother, who had raised her alone, had died only months ago. The camera had been a parting gift. Her mother said she wanted the gift to be from warm hand.

Marlane had traveled here to take photographs. But this was not just another publication assignment. Photographing the pain-carved soul of a social castaway was not even in her appointment book. This model, with his 'chewed-to-oblivion' expression, was a private matter that wouldn't yield a magazine cover. The assignment was necessary. It was personal.

"Could you tip your head up a little, please? Thanks." Marlane issued each directive with reserve. She sensed Jed's cooperation, yet concealment was within his eyes. As he moved, there was an acquiescent forfeiture. The modeling fee had been an inducement, but she couldn't hope to achieve what she wanted without allowing him his very own stage. For his suspicious sunken eyes were on the lookout for an ambush. His indigence hadn't produced any trace of acrimonious hatred. But it had given him a refugee's mistrust.

Marlane gazed at her own image in the reflective pane of glass. She appeared younger than her forty-five years. Tall, slender, her usual vivacious spirit had receded. Her attractive face was drawn. Amber eyes and high cheekbones were not cosmetically enhanced. Nor had she ever wanted to refine her slightly aquiline nose. With gleaming white teeth, her smile was a cordial flash across an angular face. There was sensuality, yet there was also a buffer zone. Long, uncontrolled beige curls framed that face.

Her expressions were normally feisty, but with a teasing quality.
Her frown was usually serene. Now, however, it was pensively
solemn. It was very nearly tense. She was on a rapacious quest for
answers. Her crucible was to find the secrets of this bewildered, old
boozer. As she exhaled a swaying sigh, she realized her pilgrimage
was to chase a sprinting shadow of the past. No wonder she felt
drained beyond the morning's jet ride from Dallas to Cincinnati.

Jed bunched back into his squat. Lanky arms wrapped his stick-
figure body. Sagging in slumberous detachment, his six-two stance
crouched against the sooty brick building. He lifted his collar to brace
the slap of wind that swirled trash and leaf confetti.

Autumn's conversion into winter chilled him. His bony hands,
with sinking tendons, became knots jamming one hand into the other.
Jed's fists tangled as if they were winding a skein of yarn. They
extended from frayed herringbone sleeves of a jacket long ago
discarded.

"You payin' me twenty-five bucks and hour?" he trawled for
reassurance.

"As we agreed, I am. Yes," she confirmed. "When we've
finished and you've signed a model release, I'll pay you in cash."
Bitterly, she thought about his concerns. They differed from her
mundane worries. Monetary concerns were his. Her concerns were a
far different agenda.

Studying him, Marlane was snared by the plundering of her own
fantasies. Reality had punctured the idea she'd had of who Jed was.
Perhaps, she thought, she'd hoped for something redeeming about
him. She focused on a human being who was nearly a nonentity. He
wasn't even comedic enough to entice the pity of a clown wearing a
bum's costume. Nor was he tragic enough to dampen her eyes.

He was a man much older than his mid-sixties portrayed him.
Leather-skinned, his face had the look of rotted fruit. Clay-red bags
were beneath bland ebony eyes. Those eyes were filmy lanterns. His
sleep-matted lashes were heavily lidded. A thorny, stubbly beard was
now nearly all gray.

No, she admitted, Jed was not some idyllic, hallowed sage. He
was a vagabond inside a less than pristine carcass. She had found
him. Now, she was attempting to know as much as he would allow.
Also as much as the afternoon would grant.

Trust, she realized, must be extracted through a dialogue of
discovery. She knew how to make his eyes flicker slightly. "Twenty-

five dollars an hour is standard for this kind of modeling fee."

She queried her motives. The self-accounting did little to soothe her. She questioned this hasty trip from her home in Dallas. Was she here because she had recently turned forty-five? It was more likely that it was because her mother had died. Maybe, she speculated, she had finally been filled with curiosity. Full disclosure was made in a letter her mother had given the lawyer. It was given to Marlane upon her mother's death. The pertinent information stated that her mother had changed her name back to her maiden name. It had been given to her infant daughter.

Wrapping her tapered fingers around the camera's body, Marlane continued shooting. After looking up, and into his face, she quickly began photographing again. She had purposely only brought one camera. She stopped from time to time to fiddle with the settings. It was a ploy for time.

Lighting changed as ragged clouds drowsily drifted. Squinting, Marlane automatically continued shooting. Her mind raced backward. Laura encouraged her to seek out her past. Laura had used her own journalistic skills in tracking down Jed. Jed's disability checks were being sent to a boarding house in Cincinnati. After getting the address, it was only a matter of a quick flight, car rental, and Marlane arrived. She'd located Jed Ellison, promised him payment, and with a skeptical nod, he'd accepted.

Marlane glanced away, resting her eyes. Slowly, she resumed. Jed's glare seemed to defiantly lock out questions that hadn't yet been asked.

He scratched his head. Mumbling, he spoke, "Sorry, I moved. No one ever paid me just to take my picture." With a gravely laugh, he added, "I'm sure no pinup." His cracked lips creased. Inside were stained, yellowed teeth. Several on one side were gone. His mouth was depressed with a concavity of the fleshy socket. It provided a one-sided smile. "Guess if I'm makin' twenty-five an hour, them handsome pinups in the fashion books must be makin' really big money."

"Far more than the photographer," Marlane agreed. She watched as Jed's sinewy hands wobbled toward a multicolored stocking cap. Rolled over his ears, the cap was mashing down straggles of hair. Jed pulled the cap from his head. His fingers combed the tousled mane. Marlane spoke, "You make a good subject." There was warmth in her voice that she hadn't counted on. She then conjectured that it was her way of relating to a person she was photographing. This was not meant to be a family reunion.

"Subject," he repeated. "That's what they called me back in the war once. I got wounded. They called me a subject. Funny, huh? I figured they thought I was some kinda royal subject. Not a patient. Did some tests on my lungs. Got me a Purple Heart for bein' all shot up."

"Tell me about it?"

"War. Well, after I was well enough they sent me stateside. Met my wife while I was recuperating. She was the prettiest nurse I ever seen. Like an angel, she was."

"Your wife?" she probed.

"Yep. She was a good woman. Left me after we was married a year. I wasn't too settled down." After a weighty pause, he quizzed, "Got yourself a husband?"

Their glance cabled. "No. Actually, I have problems making relationships work. I was raised by my mother. It was a one parent home." Her teeth clenched for a moment before continuing. "I don't believe relationships can last with any degree of happiness. I mistrust everyone who tries to enter my life. I'm unable to bond." Marlane thought about Laura's devotion. She'd been patient and understanding for several years of on-and-off again dating. "I'm lesbian," Marlane divulged.

"'Cause of bein' from a broken home?" Jed showed no signs of shock about her lifestyle disclosure.

"No. I don't believe it works that way. But it probably did impact my ability to settle down."

"Maybe you're too independent to settle down."

"Is that why you didn't settle down?"

"I shouldda never married. Even drank too much back then." As if excavating the past, he remained silent. Poised in the shadow of his awning hand, he disclosed, "I used to play guitar and sing. For tips, drinks. Well, I come back from a gig and she was gone. Ups and writes this note sayin' she was tired of traveling. It wasn't a life for her. She was tired of the road. Of me. Wanted to go back to her family."

Quickly Marlane inquired, "May I see your Purple Heart?" She speculated that might give her more time. It would also be a chance to see his room. She wanted to glean some understanding of this stranger.

"I'd show it, but it got swiped. Pawned it once. When I finally got it back, I got mugged. That's when I got a couple teeth knocked outta my head. These fellas busted up my guitar tryin' to get to my wallet. Fought 'em for that Purple Heart. Still got my other medals though."

"Maybe I could see them," she coaxed.

"They're back in my room." Sorrow raided his expression. "My place ain't fancy. I got me a little room in trade for doin' fix-ups around the building. Sweep up. Little snow-shoveling."

"Might I shoot some photos in your room? With your medals?"

"Payin' me for it?"

"The meter is running. I like to get to know my subjects. I have a theory that we all somehow imprint one another's lives when we meet people. We overlap and we influence."

With a hide-and-seek glance, he offered his riposte. "My theory is that we're each a spinning star and the galaxy is a roulette wheel." Then with a playful chuckle, he calculated, "I met me all the imprinting shits I want to. Pardon my language."

"Shits like the ones who took your medal?"

"Yeah." Puffs of swollen pockets under his eyes appeared to sink as he closed his eyelids. Wavering, he then opened them. Their glance tagged. "Guess life ain't so bad. I just never got myself tamed out." Shrugging, with a bristling orb of his shoulders, he gave a delusory salute. "I give it my best fight. But I got me drunked up a few times too many."

"Is that why you're down here?" she grilled. Her ease made the question nonchalant. She knew immediately he wasn't the type to allow her or anyone to pry his mind. Or to take his accounting.

"Guess I'm really here 'cause I don't want to be owned. On the streets, you ain't owned. Never need to worry about bein' runner-up. No overlords and no competition."

"And that makes you happy?"

"I settle for patches of contentment." He began walking.

She quickly stuffed her camera into her shoulder tote, and then scurried after him. The city smelt of exhaust fumes, oil, and trash. She studied his wandering plod as he aimlessly shifted from foot to foot. His rumpled clothing seemed to be his outer layer, she thought. She didn't identify with him. There were no echoes of her lineage. And yet, there seemed to be the requirement of knowing him. Of learning about this stranger.

Marlane wished his Purple Heart hadn't been stolen.

* * *

Footsteps reverberated as they clattered. The two trudged a vacant hallway. Off to one side was a galvanized pail with the residue of soap foam along its edges. There was an eerie stillness until Jed rattled his keys. The door groaned open. His room held a cot, wardrobe, card table with two chairs, and an empty egg crate. Atop the crate was a row of tattered books. Marlane squinted to see the names on the spines. Poe, Homer, Longfellow, Dickinson, Emerson, and Frost were among the poets. Her glance snagged on a book about Native Americans.

"I've always been interested in Native Americans," she commented, pointing to the book.

"My grandmomma was Indian. She lived on a reservation 'til my grandpop married her. Off they went together. When I was eleven, my momma dies. My daddy runs off. I went back to Oklahoma and lived with the grand folks 'til I was sixteen. Grandmomma taught me the best she could." With his words, it seemed his secrets were melting. "Still remember her cornbread and Cherokee stew. All steamin' hot. Anyways, at sixteen, I went off to make it on my own."

"Playing the guitar?"

"Naw, that came later," he answered with a wince. "Later when I got into working bars. Did some short-order cooking for a while back then. War comes up and I quit and go off to fight." Jed ducked, missing the light that snaked down from its wire. He motioned for her to be seated opposite him at the stained card table. She gathered her camera near, poised to snap at any occasion.

"I'd like to see your medals. And do you have old photos?" she prompted.

Perplexed, he asked, "What you interested in me for?"

"Photos show nerve endings. The camera captures every corner of the heart. Old photos help me gather insight." She saw the window ledge. Crumpled bread crumbs were scattered for a bird's feast. "You enjoy watching birds?"

"Naw. Just can't stand to see 'em cold and hungry. I been cold and hungry." After a pause, he asked, "Your family from Dallas?"

"Yes. My mother finally settled there when I was small. She died recently." She felt her eyes misting.

"Bet you wonder why your momma dies and a worthless old bum like me lives on."

Marlane broke their tethered gaze. She inspected the wastebasket. It was filled with potato chip sacks and bottles. The neck of an empty wine bottle lifted from the trash. "Life isn't always fair. Death doesn't go by merit."

"I'll show you my medals now," he grumbled.

She took her camera in hand. Jed placed a shoebox on the table between them. He opened it and began lifting tarnished medals. As if emptying his past, he shook his head. He rubbed a medal against his jacket. She snapped a photo as he closely inspected it.

Intent on capturing a moment of his relishing the touch of his medals, she commented, "You must be proud of being decorated?"

"Yep. When I was a young fella, I didn't know that war was no place for sissies."

He reverentially replaced the medals. His face reflected a stab of disappointment. There was silence, as if his soul was being wrenched. The pause told Marlane that he was peering into his own misfortune. "Yep," he repeated. "Death is the punch line of war." With a skeletal stiffness, he disclosed, "This hero business tricks us. I been jabbed with a bayonet. Took shells in my chest. My buddy…" the words hooked in his throat. "My buddy, he was killed saving three of us."

Quietly, he sorted photos. Sifting betrayed dreams. Marlane sensed he was allowing her to near his secret's center. "I'm sorry for your loss."

"Damn, that hurt." He fanned black and white photos across the table. He lifted one and murmured, "Loving can also take you hostage. Sometimes your soul gets all pilfered by a woman you love. She was magic to me." He handed the picture to Marlane as if surrendering it. "My wife. She give me happiness. I didn't know what to do with it."

It was incongruous. The twisting inside Marlane made her very core ice over. The photo was of her mother in the arms of a strange young man. The image stunned her.

There was a youthful, clean-cut Jed. And his arms were around the woman he loved. Marlane scrutinized her mother's young face.

She recalled the letter her mother had written. Those words barely registered then. The story was of a young couple. The woman had married a dashing guitarist, a war hero. He was like no one she'd ever known. But soon, she realized she could never know him. Marlane was shocked when she'd first read the letter. The contents were news to her. Her mother explained that she'd divorced when she found out she was pregnant. She'd left her husband with only a note explaining her invading fears. The letter expressed concern about Jed's wandering lifestyle. It was no way to bring up a child.

Traversing time, the sum of it had brought Jed here. Still only riddles told of him. Shreds and hints evaporated with a smile - then a blink.

Handing the photo back, she whispered, "She was lovely."

"She gave me happiness. Then ups and takes it away. Never even had the chance to tell her I could change. She wanted a family. And I couldda settled down."

Marlane carefully chauffeured her defense. "She may have had a reason. Maybe she didn't believe you could settle down."

His expression became hawkish, displaying the first glimpse of having anger left. "Maybe we're nothing but one another's gadget."

"I was only trying to say that we aren't always aware of people's motives." With a rueful side-glance, Marlane added, "She must have been proud of your war heroics."

"We about done?" He gathered the small stack of photos.

"Yes. Let's get the model release signed. Then, if you like, I'll buy you that drink promised at the corner bar." Marlane dug though her bag. She handed him the pen and form. As he took them, she slid a hundred dollar bill across the table.

"You're really goin' to the gin mill for a quick one with me? And buying?" He signed an elaborate cueiformed signature on the release.

She didn't take time to read it, but folded it and slipped it into her bag's side-pocket. "Certainly." She knew the recipe for befriending an alcoholic. Offer to buy a drink. Even though the life is to become social litter, a free drink is the sacrosanct folly.

Marlane paused. She skirmished with thought about being a byproduct of sperm and egg. Humanity is the winding ballad of DNA.

Introspectively she watched as Jed topped his shoebox with the hundred dollar bill packed inside. The box was carefully tucked inside a drawer.

A few of his aged photographs were placed in a small book. He then placed the book in his coat pocket.

Marlane considered that no matter how independent we are, we search a nest where we are safe, and where our treasured belongings are secure. And perhaps, she thought, we search rescues. He, however, was done searching. Jed was an absentee progenitor. He wasn't seeking resolution. She was the searcher. She had wanted to tell him. She wanted to let him know that because he wasn't there, her life had been damaged. Also to tell him she tasted loneliness each time she swallowed. But that oration was no longer important to her.

They walked the hallway. Inhaling the strong cleaning compound sickened her. She was relieved when they stepped onto the sidewalk.

With a burst of excitement, he declared, "We can go on down to the corner."

"Yes, the corner," she recited.

* * *

"Walt Whitman's my favorite. He was the first and maybe last non-whore this country's literary folks produced," Jed announced. He gulped down a shot of whiskey, and then sipped a sudsy beer. "He had purity. He wasn't no prostitute of spirit."

"It's rather beyond our control to be owned by society," Marlane countered. "For instance, if you continue talking with me, I might spring for another boilermaker. Right?" she dueled with a slight smile.

And elusive twist of his hand became a fluttering wing wave. To the barmaid, he said, "I think the pretty lady just offered to buy another round."

Looking around at the dive, Marlane felt its griminess. "Nothing more for me though," Marlane joked. "I've got to be clear headed to drive to the airport."

Mocking her soft drink, Jed grumbled, "Thought soda pop was for kids."

Gazing into his waxen face, she realized he was still a stranger. His grizzle spirit had only given up partial information. He was at home here. Here with the smoke fumes, the stale aroma of beer and perspiration, dilapidated booths, and aged floorboards.

She rummaged her mind. She would be arriving in Dallas late. She would probably miss this evening's AA meeting. Laura had teased that she would go for Marlane and take notes. But Laura didn't have the problem. Laura wanted nothing more than to be a part of the solution.

Marlane had grudgingly entered the program in hopes that something might stabilize her. She'd told herself for ten years that she needed a drink to ease the stress of her profession. There were split-second decisions connected with being a photographer – a photojournalist. Deadlines pressed. To be social, she'd offered her own absolution. Meeting and greeting were difficult. A couple drinks and she was gregarious and outgoing. And then there was that old excuse about being more creative. Her work was with free abandon when she'd tipped a few. Also, of course, that included a sad trail of lovers. And one more drink for the road.

"Jed," she uttered. Moments seemed perishable. Just as all bygone moments, this one would soon be pleated into a cluster of others. Memories. Time, left behind by *now*. "I'm glad I got to know you. Truly glad."

"You ain't a bad kid," Jed muttered. He lifted his glass. "Here's to your mother and my lost buddy." Their gaze locked. Their glasses clanked. Blinking, he reached into his pocket and pulled out a worn copy of *Leaves of Grass*. He handed it across the table. His words were strained. "My eyes are goin' out on me. Thought you might like this book. My favorite."

"Thank you." She placed it in her huge purse. After a final sip, she felt the silence. As if landmines had been strategically placed around her, she hesitated when she stood. She tossed a couple of twenties on the table. "This should cover the bar tab. I'll think of you when I read the book. I promise, I'll think of you."

Jed Ellison took another gulp from the shot glass. She swung her bag over her shoulder. He muttered his inaudible thanks. He then returned his attention to his drink.

She exited without a final glance backward. Slowly, she slipped into the rental car. As she pressed the key into its ignition, she remembered the book. She took it from her pocket and opened it to where a small ribbon bookmark was place. She read the underscored words aloud. "And again I walk'd the beach under the paling stars of morning. My ties and ballasts leave me, my elbows rest in sea-gaps, I skirt sierras, my palms cover continents, I am afoot with my vision."

Closing the book, her eyes filled and her arms folded into an oval around the steering wheel. She rested her head against the fingers that gripped the top of the wheel. She sobbed against her life preserver. There was a sense of abandonment.

Marlane wasn't certain *who* the enigmatic stranger really was. He was someone who had married too young. He was a person who had no more answers than she did. Sniffing, she checked her image in the rearview mirror. She didn't resemble either her mother or her father. Nor did she look to be a combination of them.

She wondered why she'd pursued this. Perhaps out of a sense of inquiry - born of the spirit of a seeker. Maybe time required it of her. The probability was that Laura had prodded her. Laura would do anything to help the woman she loved. Laura, Marlane mused. Her thoughts jumped into a tangling panic. Laura. What if she was just another woman who wanted to own her very soul? To own Marlane?

Marlane quickly lifted the model release from her bag. She unfolded it to see the Whitmonian flair with which it was signed: *Sing a visionary's song.* She then again picked up the book - *Leaves of Grass.* The photos slid out – they'd been enclosed. She held them to her heart.

He knew all the time, she deduced. Today was as much of her heritage as she was likely to get from him. She turned the ignition key. Her strength was siphoned. Nothing was in focus. She'd captured the landmarks in photographs, she lamented. And this stopover had provided many landmarks within a face.

To herself, she stated that heroism doesn't need to last to have been. Perhaps he didn't know until now. Now – when it was too late for anything but complete forgiveness. He may have tried. And of course Jed Ellison is owned. All visionaries are owned.

And of course Marlane loved Laura. She wanted to be the woman worthy of Laura's love. One day she would be able to accept a loving relationship.

But for now, she would work on one visionary word from one spinning star at a time. If the plane arrived early, and she hurried, she could make her meeting.

Photograph by Kathie Solie

X-CHROMOSOMES

"That's the ticket," Dolly Riggs reassured. She leaned down to give the child's plump cheek a soft tweak. "A smile is better than a frown any old day. Why you do have a sweet little face when it's smiling, Violet. Your name suits you. For a fact, it does." Standing back, Dolly gave a frisky nod toward the five-year old. "We all like happy endings"

Violet Thomas blinked into the sun. She focused her squint on the spry octogenarian. One of the neighbors had called Dolly Riggs a senile old bat of dubious sexual leanings. Miss Agatha Dillard, her dear friend and *housemate*, had died two years ago. Dolly had shared a home with Miss Agatha for over fifty years. Everyone on the block called the two women spinsters. Some, however, were more graphic. Violet had no earthly idea what 'leps-beings' were. And her mother told her it wasn't of any true importance anyway.

To Violet, Dolly was only a nice old neighbor lady. She wore strange garb. A huge pagoda straw hat was always worn in the sun. Along with long-sleeved shirts and pants, because Miss Agatha had always said that Dolly had a bad way with the sun. Dolly's wardrobe may have set her apart as eccentric, but even that seemed to endear her to the children on the block. She always had time for them. She took time to give them apples from her giant apple tree. She also told them the story of Joanie Appleseed. That was the feminist version, naturally. *And* she insisted the kids call her by her first name, rather than Mrs. Riggs. That title annoyed her.

"Davey run off with my favorite seashell. Aunt Lana brought it from the ocean. Brought it special for me. And Davey stole it," Violet tattled with a grumble inside her jaw.

When her parents divorced, Aunt Lana had moved in with Violet and her mother, Jody. Aunt Lana was a traveling business woman. She often went near the ocean, and always brought a special shell and a t-shirt for Violet.

"Why on earth would Davey do that?" Dolly quizzed. "The boy has more toys than sense. He's as selfish as the day is long. Why his big brother never acted like that. He was a gentleman. But that Davey!"

"Well, he did it. He *took* it offa me. To be mean, I 'spose," Violet incriminated her playmate. She gave a sway of her curly blonde locks to confirm the crime.

"Never thought I'd see the day when he could get one over on you, Violet Rae Thomas."

"He did it to be spiteful. Aunt Lana tells that Davey is a spiteful little shit if ever there was one. And my mom says Aunt Lana knows character. Why Aunt Lana even told

Mommy that my Daddy wasn't right for her. Mom says I was the only good thing that come outta getting married. But she had to try marriage on."

"Lots of folks don't pick the right flavor first off."

"Aunt Lana says she's amazed my dad didn't goof up with a Y."

"A *Y*?" Dolly questioned, gawking down at the child.

"Yes. Instead of the X-chromosome."

Dolly grinned. "Aunt Lana said that, did she?"

"Yep. Now, how am I gonna get my shell back?"

"Why that's clear as a fresh scrubbed window." Dolly's frown broke. Memory, she mused, is where our past is reinvented. She found similarities in most events trailing from her many yesterdays. "One time I wanted something that was taken from me. I set my mind thinking and came up with a plan."

"Criminy sakes," Violet squealed. "I just need me a plan."

"Can't use my exact plan. It's been used up by me. But we can change it about." She crossed her spindly arms defiantly. Leaning down, she asked, "Want to try that?"

"Sure. You come up with good plans."

"You'll need to be clever as all get-out." Dolly hesitated. "Solving problems can usually be done in one of two ways. Blossoms or bullets."

"Blossoms and bullets?" Violets face squeezed with pure bewilderment. "What's that all about?"

"Blossoms, well, that's giving folks a smile. You serve Davey up some teacakes and sugar."

"Dave is too spoiled for that business. His momma bakes a bunch."

Dolly reconsidered, "Well, I mean by being kindly to him, but I do believe he's far too strong-willed for blossoms to work." She dipped the brim of her hat. "Blossoms are out."

"I got no bullets," Violets whined with a shrug. "I don't even have me a gun."

"Bullets don't mean real bullets. It means you use tactics that aren't so kindly."

"That'll get me in Dutch at Sunday school." With a puffy sigh, she asked, "What did you have so you needed a blossoms or bullet plan?"

"My best friend wanted my beau. I married him. Thought I would have a family of sweet little ones. That never came to be. Anyways, my friend still wanted him. So I gave him to her. I sort of traded for her roommate. Well, she regretted the trade. And I never regretted it for one minute." Dolly cackled. "Not one minute of my whole life."

Violet's lips protruded. "I want my shell back," she brayed. She stomped her foot. "And I'm gonna get it, too. Aunt Lana said not to be in-tim-a-dated. Not by him, or any other boy in the world. She tells me never try to be equal to boys 'cause that would be lowering my standards. She says I'm already better because of my X business makin' me a little girl."

"What's your mama say?" Dolly quizzed with amusement.

"She says Aunt Lana is a radical, separatist, feminist Sapphic."

"Gracious," Dolly said with a bolt. "But that's your little secret."

"I got another secret, too."

Dolly's eyebrows lifted. "I'll bet I can guess."

"You can?"

"I'll bet your Aunt Lana *isn't* really your aunt. But she's a pretend aunt."

"How'd you know?"

"Just a *wild* guess."

"Yeah, but I can't tell anybody. Besides, Aunt Lana is the best aunt I could have anyway."

"Yes. Now then, little Violet, what do you intend on doing about your special shell?"

"This blossom and bullet tactic isn't for me," the small girl answered. "I'm gonna give Davey a shake or two. Smack him in the tummy if I got to. That should do the trick. Aunt Lana said it was okay to tear a strip offa him. An' I'm gonna do just that."

Violet stormed down the sidewalk. Pure determination was her ally. Dolly shook her head and snickered for many moments. She watched until Violet was out of sight. Then she returned to tending her begonias. Dolly fussed over her flowers with the tenderness they deserved. Several times she put down her garden shovel and chuckled to herself.

"X-chromosomes, indeed!"

Kieran York

YESTERYEAR LYRICIST: HER POETRY OF US

Noonday's Greeting:

With apprehensive veneration, I voyaged across the Aegean Sea toward Lesbos. My head was bowed with humility as I thought of interviewing Sappho.

Bevin, I cautioned myself with a nervous lecture, *she may not be the woman you've envisaged.*

Sappho is more than a celebrity. She is the great, unrivaled woman poet of Lesbos. She is the weaver of music and lyrics. She is the inventor - the creator, of Sapphic stanzas. She has put fire in her verses.

I have been granted an interview. Me, a scribe from across many seas, would soon be in her presence. Bevin, the translator – birthed from Celtic tribes of warrior women. Shy Bevin, descended from women of the Iron Age – I considered my plight.

I had traveled far. It had been a treacherous and difficult journey. But that was of little consequence. For this wayfaring was the most important travel of my existence.

My language skills from my own Brittonic and Celtic based tongue had translated many of the renowned woman's songs. Now I am to be the correspondent responsible for bringing the women of my homeland information about the world's greatest poet. Also, I would complete the translations of all her work. Then scribes would be able to provide the libraries of my land with Sappho's magnificence.

Hence, I - Bevin, shall prepare to visit Lesbos, the isle of young women and their famous mentor – Sappho of Lesbos, Greece.

As with my own ancestral homeland's native tongue, the Aeolian culture of Sappho's is rich with words. Lesbos is recognized as the jewel of the entire Hellenic civilization. Its most notable citizen is known throughout the poetry world. I've read and memorized much of Sappho's great works. In my land, I'd heard the oracles sing her famous odes. Those lyrics were etched upon my heart. I had been captured by the celestial recitations. Her vividly visceral style roamed through my dreams.

I found Sappho's songs to be warm and natural. Their lyrical messages expressed her affection, despair, reverence for life, as well as passion for love. Many claimed that her skills were far greater than the ancient poet, Homer, as well as her contemporary, Alcaeus.

There was the realization that I must know the poetess in flesh and blood to best interpret her work, to translate those lovely lyrics, and tell of her in my homeland. Now, just as in a dream I'd had many months ago, I was going to her. This great merchant vessel was wending its way toward Greece – toward her. The sails flailed in the breeze. The gulls above glided, and shrieked of my arrival.

I, Bevin, was aboard this ship. I, Bevin, would soon know Sappho.

When I neared my destination, there was great trepidation. I could hear the raging surf, crashing against craggy rocks. My body tensed. I reached to check my hair. A tiara of braided hair, with a saffron-colored fillet, was crowning my head. Blonde, with sun streaks, my locks of hair draped down onto my shoulders. My hands reached to tap roses onto my pale cheeks.

A quick glance down to check my Celtic linen *chiton* told me that my cloud-white, long tunic was presentable. Fabric dipped from my bare shoulder and was gathered by a gold ring at my opposite shoulder. My sandals were elaborately decorated with the embroidery of my country. Around my neck hung a golden disk that clung to my collarbone – my prized *tork*. Gold armlets circled my upper arms. The dress I'd selected was of my Hallstatt culture. I hoped the jewelry was not too garish for her sensibilities.

Filled with self-consciousness, I hoped that Sappho would overlook my faults. I longed for her to warmly receive me. I am in my early twenties, too old to be a youth under the tutelary. These younger women will complete her finishing school and become wives of famous royalty, merchants, and war commanders. Her academy for young women has been renowned for years. Two of her pupils had become most famous, as well. Erinna of Telos and Damophyla of Pamphylia were well-recognized.

On the Isle of Lesbos, the young women of marriageable age studied grace. Called *charis*, the curriculum consisted of art, dancing, poetry, philosophy, and romantic endeavors. Sappho's young disciples were gifted with the teachings of their aristocratic, refined educator.

Again, the shiver caused by my own lack of training was overwhelming me. Although properly educated, my tutelage was without elegance, culture, and delicacy. Those elements of womanhood had not been unfolded.

Here, I acknowledged, I am in the vestibule of exquisite and ennobled gentility. I was lacking the grace of these women. For what if Sappho - a woman rich with artistic spirit, an illustrious personage with inimitable grace –found me unintelligent or uninteresting? Would her witty sarcasm banish me from Lesbos?

She was now in her late twenties, and had just lost the love of young Atthis to Andromeda. Certainly, her soul would yet weep for her lover. I hoped this visit of a young translator would not be intrusive. These were my considerations as we debarked from the ship and made our way to Sappho's residence.

From the street there was the scent of burning myrrh, cassia, and frankincense. Each footstep was made with enormous reverence. For this was my life's finest odyssey. Remembrances would be indelible and last each moment of my existence.

As I followed behind her attendant, I nearly collapsed with apprehension when I saw the limestone buildings. I could see the marble inner colonnades as we approached. We entered. Enchanted, I felt the warm wrap of the frescoed walls. Vases, with her words printed, and an artist's rendering, were on a table very near the small shine to Aphrodite. I wondered if the likeness was true. Many months ago, when I first made my request to see Sappho, I had viewed a small statue of the poetess. It had been brought to my land.

There was much beauty within the statuary, but as I turned to witness the great woman herself, I realized no painting or sculpture could equal her loveliness. There was such radiance. I needed to recapture my breath. She gazed back into my face and extended her hands.

I trembled when those magnetic, midnight eyes glowed on me. She sensed my weakness, and came to my side. As her hands enwrapped mine, she leaned to kiss each of my cheeks. I inhaled the floral fragrance of her. The warmth of her body soothed as she pressed nearer.

"Bevin," she said my name. Her voice, with Aeolic dialect, bewitched me with its softness. It was with an authoritative strength. Yet, her words made my name a song -perhaps a ballad of day. "I welcome you to Lesbos. Bevin, your name is divine."

"Bevin means melodious lady. However my voice is not that of my namesake – Bevin. For she was a woman with a lovely voice. Folktales say even the birds stopped to listen when she sang. Just as your voice is magnificent, hers was also."

Before I could thank her for the praising of my name, she spoke. "Such a long voyage, your heart must feel to be a vagabond."

"My travels were wondrous, for I knew they would bring me to your side." I questioned, "Do you enjoy travel?"

"Ah, at times. I travel the realm much more now. At one time, however, I was exiled from Mytilene. Because of civil unrest, my family was banished to Sicily. You see, it was a time of feuding aristocrats and political turmoil and many were exiled. Home is belonging. In my heart there is the home that belongs to me and to all those I love. When I compose, I am on holiday. I write within the holiday of home."

"Mytilene is a magnificent land."

"It is the most important of the five major cities of Lesbos. I proudly call it my home."

Her smile was a lustrous bloom as she led me first to the grand hall. I noted that she was much more delicate than I had imagined. Petite, with a full, lovely formed body, her carriage was upright, yet she flowed as she walked. She wore a milk-white *chiton*. Folds of the gown spilled down to hide her ankles. On her feet were stylish ox hide sandals. From her shoulders draped a blazing sapphire-colored robe. Behind her, the robe's waves shifted as Sappho moved.

Her dark, flowing curls of ebon hair were pulled back from a noble face. A diadem crowned her forehead as it circled to the back of her head where those curls were wound. Several curls hung from her temples, framing her face. Her olive-hued face held the sheen of vigor. Her skin was flawless. Dark eyes gleamed expressively – gently. Her nose was strong, imposing, and finely balanced with her face. Her lips were carnelian red, and captivated me with a lush smile.

"Your isle is beyond beauty," I timidly praised.

"Yes. I shall show you my wondrous island. Each corner is filled with love. That includes our gardens, vineyards, fields, and the temple."

"It would be lovely to see it all. Perhaps I might interview you as we walk?"

"Yes, of course you may." Our eyes met. My heart raced as she said, "Your knowledge of the Greek language is delightful. So please interview me as much as you like."

"Thank you. I appreciate your gracious offer to allow me to better know you. I pray that my language skill is adequate to translate

your poems for the women in my homeland." I added my admission,"
I also wished to be in your presence so that I can better know you."

Her head tipped slightly. "I understand." When her smile
reappeared, she took my hand in hers. My explanation had satisfied
her. For she knew instinctively my reasons were varied, and deeply
felt. Her touch was warm and gentle as no other touch I'd ever felt or
might have imagined.

As we wandered the paths of Lesbos, we shared the afternoon's
blaze of light. Each footprint left behind had its own historic message.
I was learning this woman's glory with each meter.

My heart had certainly been surrendered by the time we reached
a ledge of the ocean. Looking over the panorama of great marble
cliffs and rushing waters, I recounted the sites she had shown me.

We had visited the altars of the deities. Aphrodite and the Muse
at the Temple enchanted me. We had examined wall friezes, and she
had explained their tributes and meanings to me. It was vital, she
insisted, that her ardent followers aspire to find wisdom in their lives.
If not, they would be unable to cultivate lyrics and music. Poetry
required that.

It was also crucial that each woman care properly for her health.
Sappho divulged how she had insisted that athletics be taught. She
added, boasting with a smile, that she had coached many champion
runners. "My favorite game is racing. Many of my students excel.
There are other varieties of champions, as well," she added with a
raised eyebrow. "A woman's charm is multifaceted. For we are
complex, intricate, and part of our wonder is surprise itself."

I told her I didn't doubt it for an instant. Together we laughed as
she alluded to the mysteries of womanhood. The woman I had
believed to be inaccessible was not so at all.

When the conversation dwindled, I asked, "May I inquire of your
past?" I interviewed as we walked.

"Certainly. My birthplace was Eresus. During my childhood I
lived in an elegant home of prosperity. Although luxurious, I was
taught that wealth without worthiness is no fine companion."

"Your family?"

"I have three brothers. Larichus, the youngest, is quite honored
to be a cupbearer in the town hall. Charaxus is a wine merchant, and
is somewhat estranged. A woman called Doricha was at the center of
our disagreement. My other brother is called Eurygyus."

"I have been told that you married."

"In my youth. Yes. At the time most of the younger men were

away at war. There was an older man my family deemed suitable. As is the custom, I was married. He was an affluent merchant called Kerhylas of Andros. He died soon after, leaving me with one daughter, Cleis. I named my child after my dear mother."

"That is a very great tribute."

"My life has been one of much luxury, yet I have seen strife and hardship as well."

"Your poetry reflects knowledge of both heartache and enormous love."

Passing by a field of young women, she shooed them away. "Go now, my little *hetairai*." To me she whispered, "My young companions would follow after me all afternoon, if I allowed it. But I must show you my special locations. Here, beneath the sun, on this glorious isle, my body lives. My heart's soul resides within the love I offer. My songs also reside." She pointed, "Within my library my words are stored. I have words copied for you and the women of your land."

"I thank you for entrusting me and my homeland with your lyrics." I gazed at the building. "What a lovely spot and structure."

"My library is filled with many papyrus scrolls. My education, my thought, and my expression all exist here. I've written my words on papyri. Many scribes have copied each of my books. In all, I have nine books. Those are epigrams, elegeas, lyric monodies, and so on." She laughed. "My devoted enthusiasts would say that I write not only from my intellect, but from my emotion. My critics would say the same. To critics, I say let maledictions take them."

"Is there any better way to write than from one's emotion?" I joined her laughter. "Yes, it is true, as with your writing, there is much wit and wisdom."

"I can't imagine writing without wit and wisdom brought forth by emotions. Without the truth of emotion – how can words be extracted from the heart?"

"I find your fervid verse as fresh as the blossom's breath."

"Ah, yes. But I can also write many acerbic words. And they often mingle with bittersweet poetry."

"It is so." Her secrets were being shared. My fortune was astounding. "Thank you for sharing this with me."

"Come along, Bevin. There is so much more to show you." Her exuberance bubbled, "So very much."

My smile unfolded as we stood together on a small, rocky

mound. We heard voices. Looking behind us, we turned to watch her entourage of young women romping in the background. I could understand her retinue of young women and their worship of her. They would follow her, as would I. For only in this short time, with such a brief glimpse of her, I recognized the enduring impression of this multi-faceted, esteemed woman.

These women knew her far better than I. She was exalted, adored, and celebrated by them all. Certainly the world knew her distinguished and acclaimed words – but these women honored her womanhood.

Watching them, I could see joy. Some of the women's faces were veiled as they frolicked. Some were with garlands wreathing around their heads. The garlands were of ivy, rosebuds, braided violets, pansies, wild parsley, dill sprigs, and other assorted wildflowers that they'd weaved. They held hands as they circled in a dance. Flounced skirts ruffled in the breeze. Performing for the Goddesses, they twirled while their honey-voices sang with melodic intensity.

"Their voices are the songs of nightingales," Sappho related. "What sweetness there is within our celebration!"

When we had passed beyond the women, we entered a location where an arch of perfumed rosebuds bloomed. Sappho pointed to the pink cliff roses. "The Gallic rose is said to have been colored by Aphrodite's blood," she divulged.

I inhaled the nearby sweet scent of small spicy white flowers. "Such fragrance – it is the perfume of spring."

"Myrtle," she identified. "And your heart is springtime."

When our gaze met, I awkwardly said, "Your garden is exquisite. You are truly the very icon of love."

She pointed out the floral blue against the back of the area. She noted, "Across the garden is a wall of larkspur. They match your eyes. I shall forever view them, and see your eyes in my remembrance."

My throat was too dry to speak. Yet, there was nothing I could have said. I simply nodded in her direction.

I then turned to go beyond the arch – into another terrace garden that overlooked the sea. There was complete seclusion and silence. A current of air gently swayed the olive branches. Surrounding us were also fig and bay trees. Their fragrances lifted and mingled with the oleander, wild pomegranate, honey-clover, sweet-briar, and nearby apple groves and pine-tree coves.

In the center of the garden was a marble fountain with sculpted water nymphs. Sparkling droplets above the waves lifted, and became music when hitting the water below.

Sappho's lovely voice shared, "Often it is believed that if one is afforded the luxuries and elegancies of life, one's appreciation for simplicity wanes. For me, a wreath of simple flowers, perhaps wild rosemary and violets, is as lovely as a golden crown. A lifting field of flowers is preferred to the grandeur of statues and frescoes."

"I do agree. I understand the verity of your wisdom."

"I wish only to impart wisdom to the youthful maidens of my academy. They must honor themselves. For Aeolian woman mix freely with male society, and must be educated.

I reached to touch a chervil bloom as I passed by pots of flowers. "Your gardens are exquisite. They must, along with Aphrodite, the Graces, and the golden Muses, inspire you."

"They must indeed, for I wish to inspire youth to chant and sing, and also to think. We are all in a sacred Sorority of Thiasos. This includes my companions, Atthis, Telesippa, and Megara. My best pupils - Anogora, Meletus, Gongyla, and Anactoria, must be well-rehearsed for living in this world of intellect. I wish for my companions, *hetaerae* - to belong to the world as wise and strong women. I want them to be like white meliot – honey-clover. Soft, and yet unyielding."

"That is a brave aspiration." I considered the worth of women.

"There is great tension between sexes."

"Tension?" I inquired.

"The world differs greatly for women. I am intoxicated with womanhood. Men are taught to revere other men. Yet, although women have rights, we are not valued. We still must bring power and wealth to marriage. To many men we are appendages. For instance, with statuary, one might see the differences. Male statues are called *kouroi* and they are nude. Women, called *korai*, are always clothed. Marriage is often cold, without mutual desire, unlike the love of women."

Wanting to pursue her thoughts, yet bumbling with a desire not to show how enthralled I was about her, I continued with my professional interview. "And how is it you would like to be known throughout the world?"

"Ah, I wish to be known as a lyrist. I have invented Sapphic meter, style and technique. Poetry and my love of the feminine are my gifts to the world. With precious oil, I wish to anoint words with my love."

"You are revered now. You will be forever," I said knowingly.

"One day they might lampoon me."

"You speak words with such eloquence, they would never do that."

"One cannot know how history will treat us." Her eyelids closed for several moments.

"We can pray to the Goddesses," I encouraged. "Perhaps they will be the guardians of your words. I shall do all that I can to make certain your words safe."

Sappho acknowledged, "I am amazed at the great fluency of my language you've acquired. I shall be most pleased for you to act as both the translator of my work, and the emissary of me."

"Thank you. I am honored."

"I have never seen hair and skin so pale and illuminated. And your larkspur-blue eyes - they are like the sea's blueness with flecks from the silver moon."

The warmth of my blush was felt. I noted that her eyes held mystery – but paradoxically revealed the universe. Secrets, harbored in her lovely eyes, were hers alone. She leaned and picked an ivory rose cluster.

As she handed it to me, I said, "To think that someone so celebrated is also so kind. It is more than I'd hoped for," I confessed shyly. "There is so much glory within your life. I feel great homage because you've shared these moments with me."

"Yet my glory is within peril's reach!" Her eyes dulled for a brief time. "My face might be engraved on coinage, statues of me erected, and portraits that capture my likeness – but I fear it is fleeting fame. It is as temporary as the ivory-colored rose. For fame comes with thorns," she said with a sudden throaty laugh. She swatted away a honeybee. "I might also say that fame is much like a bee. For it is a delightful song in flight, but is not without a stinger attached. All of life is bittersweet. One lives for rose petals and bee's honey."

"As well as love? Is it not correct that one lives for love?"

"Most importantly – well, firstly, yes. One lives for love, and for loving. Life is an offering and love is the sweetest portion of that gift."

Moving nearer to me, within inches of my face, I witnessed the radiance of her. "You are so beautiful," I shyly commented.

"Her head lowered with thankfulness. "You are a precious soul,

Bevin. Do you have additional inquiries?"

Questioning myself, I wondered if my emotion was one of infatuation. The roses in the cup of my hands had been tenderly placed there. My heart was covered with a mantle of flowers. "Perhaps later, you must be weary of questions."

Smiling, she spoke softly, "Don't be concerned, I have a temperament that will allow you to know if I am tired of being interviewed. But I wish for you to know me. So for now it is enough of questions, but not enough of you, my darling Bevin."

Blushing, and with a tremble in my voice, I said "Again, you honor me."

Twilight's Banquet

"You are a white dove," she insisted, taking my hand in hers.

Together our footsteps took us into the banquet room. Pillows were placed beside the eighteen-inch high, long banquet table. It was decorated with multiples of flowers that strung its elongated length.

All of the young women were in their colorful, festive dress. With aigrettes, circles of bandeaus, and chaplets of dill crowning their hair, the women were gleaming with joy. But no one was as beguiling as the festive Sappho.

She was bedecked in a coral *chiton*. Her garland was woven with matching flowers. She was adorned by a golden neck chain and sparkling arm rings. Her dark, almond-shaped eyes flashed with the anticipation of this celebration.

Torches, on the walls between the friezes, cast their dim light upon her. Light reflected her grandeur, and virtue. Shadows veiled her lovely face in seclusion.

I could not help my forwardness, as we were seated. I leaned near to her and whispered, "Sappho, you are the most extraordinary woman I've ever known."

Amused, she questioned, "Is it that you know me, or wish to know me?"

"I feel that I know you through the words that you've presented to us." I paused as my cheeks warmed. "And I should like to know *you*."

A slight smiled decorated her lips. She was silent as she watched the ruby-red wine being poured into a delicately sculpted golden chalice. When the server had removed the flasks of wine, Sappho spoke. "The wine is excellent. Banquet wine is mixed with honey and spices. I believe it is our very best libation in the realm. She lifted it to her lips to sample. Then she handed the chalice to me. "Yes, it is magnificent. You must share my wine with me."

I carefully took the vessel. Slowly, I turned the rim around to where her lips had pressed – her kiss had touched. I put my lips to the edge and sipped. I tasted both the wine, and where Sappho's lips had warmly savored it. "Excellent," I agreed. "Thank you for your hospitality. I'm honored to be sharing your table, your wine, and your glorious company. I am pleased."

Clapping her hands, she directed the banquet to begin. Round, wreathed loaves of bread were served. There were enormous silver trays heaped high with olives, cheeses, baked lentils, figs, and chickpeas. Upon platters of gold were mounds of goat meat that had been baked in leaves and seasoned with herbs and olive oil. The steamy redolence lifted, as the fragrances of each spice and herb mingled.

When we had completed the feast's main course, more platters were delivered. Stacks of fruits, fresh figs and, huge globes of grapes were presented. Sappho inhaled the ambrosial aroma, and then plucked a cluster of grapes. Facing me, she pulled one from its stem. Her fingers sensually dispatched it toward my lips.

As I tenderly bit into it, juices flooded my mouth. Her lips turned upward and her eyes sparkled. "These grapes are prized for their flavor."

"And correctly so. Their flavor was given them by the Goddesses. And touched by you." My glance automatically lowered. I was certain my face was blushing.

"Now, I shall now sing a love song for you, Bevin. I dedicate my song to you, and to every woman who has ever wanted a love song dedication."

I watched while her attendants brought an assortment of musical instruments. "They are so magnificent," I praised.

"I've proudly introduced a new instrument to Lesbos. This one," she pointed out, "is the *barbitos,* a lyre with a very deep tone, and eight stings. Then there is a *magadies*, which is a harp with twenty strings, and a *kithara*. I shall perform a song for you with my own accompaniment on the tortoise-shell lyre. It is my favorite instrument, although I also play a small harp called *pectis*."

When her attendant handed her the lyre, her fingers strummed sweet sounds. Her gentle voice lulled each word, as if releasing it up into the realm of Goddesses. I memorized each lyric as she sang. Each word was a jewel in a treasure chest of precious stones. Her song requested that I open my arms and my heart to her.

Of course I would gladly lavish my desire upon her.

Evening's Seduction

The woman who had been called the tenth Muse was indeed inspiring.

She stepped away from her *chiton*. Deliberately she eased the sash from my linen robe. Her eyes flickered with the lantern's light. I felt the pause of all eternity.

Together we bathed in milk and water. Floating hyacinth blossoms covered the warm tub that was filled with scented liquid. Ceremonially, we touched, as we immersed our bodies into the bath. It was only moments after our fingers had chained when our lips met. Her kiss was softly passionate – tenderly eager. Caressing one another, I knew my heart had never felt the touch of such love. My heart was being touched with womanhood, as we caressed one another.

After bathing, we dried one another's skin. The glow of moonlight spilled against her. She stood back as she unfastened her long, dark tresses. When she released her ringlets, they fell softly against her shoulders. Their color became violet. Her arms invited me into her silken embrace.

We walked through a small torch-lit corridor to her private chambers. Before she drew the lattice closed, she pointed upward. She spoke, "The great Evening Star is Venus. We call it Hesperus."

"Tonight is ours," I replied. "Under your heavens, we share amorous embraces."

Dim lit, a candle's flirting sparks of brightness flashed against the opposite side of the room. Sweet bay and a dotting of petals scattered across the floor like whirling confetti. Dainty rosebuds were strewn the length of the downy bed. Together we lowered our bodies onto the plush, warm bed.

"Please cushion your heart against mine," she whispered tenderly. "I am famished for the pleasure of binding my love against your love. My pale dove, share my desire – and soothe the lambent flame that sears my heart and soul."

"Yes," I murmured, as we reclined our nudity of sweetness together. "Yes."

"Our glorious moon Goddess, Selene, watches over us as we share, and as we slumber." She clasped me tightly. Her hushed words spoke, "We shall tame our desires." Roaming my neck, her lips erotically glided down the length of my skin. Excitement escalated when her mouth lingered. Her fingertips traced my form with great and deliberate fervency. Passionate, tantalizing, her love was an alluring temptation.

We shared our bodies with a sensual trading of emotion. Explicit was our desire.

The night was cherished by us both.   My love journeyed to womanhood's altar. My adoration for her was enraptured reverence. Fragile, resilient, transitory, and within the great wingspan of forever – emotions were.

From the window, I heard the tangling crashes of waves as they smashed against stone cliffs. Ledges against the ocean were marble cliffs. Beneath were splashing, flushing tides. Barely audible were the bursting gusts of breeze that sang through leaves - yet I heard their lullaby. I heard the faint echoes of distant harps, and a flute mingling with the chirrup of crickets.

I would forever hear Sappho's erotic breath against my face.

Morning's Farewell

Morning's great flaxen sun awakened me. Sappho's arms circled me - and mine held her. My heart was also encircled by her.

Warmth, laughter, kindness, and pleasure swarmed us. My love had danced the brink of forever. Our intimacy was to clasp *us* for all times within the celebration of two women loving.

Counting down our final time together before I would be leaving was difficult. We breakfasted in bed. Chestnuts, fruit, and wine-dipped bread were softly fed to one another. We drank honeyed wine from the two-handled *kylix*.

Her whispered words painted my heart. "Just as Helen of Troy was abducted from her land, time is also seizing you from my side. Can you not stay?"

"My ship prepares to sail. I must return – I have given my word. I have vowed to return to them – bringing your lyrics. That was my bargain allowing me to make this journey. I must return to tell of our interview. I promised to translate your nine books of odes, *epithalamia*, elegies, and hymns. If I stay even one more day, I may never return to my homeland. My vow to women would be broken. For I have given an oath that I would reunite with my family and the women who await your poetry. I can't break my promise to those who rely on me."

She smiled benevolently. "I am glad that you know of me, as well as my words." Anguish took her thoughts for a moment. Then as if lecturing, she added, "Remember, my first book of Sapphic stanzas contain 1,320 lines."

"I shall not forget." Lifting, the corners of my lips reassured her.

"Please remember my island. Tell the women of your land that I send immortal love. I send my gift of perpetual words to them. As well as to you."

The sweetness of myrrh incense lifted. The brightness of the isle made her face glisten. "You have bestowed such grace on my life, Sappho. I and all the women of my land have now inherited your songs. You have gifted my country - gifted all women like me. Your lyrics are for all those who know you, as well as all those who will come to know you."

"Do you believe that my lyrics will endure?"

Her poetry would survive – how could it not? Her books were a catalogue of love that gave a view of each woman. They gave the touch of time and the tender emotion of our living. They gave the taste of nectar.

"I can only imagine them enduring. For your legacy has been inscribed within our bosoms. You'll always be somewhere within our hearts and our hopes."

Sappho kissed my shoulder. Then she brushed my hair gently. "My dove, Bevin, do you truly believe that I shall be in the remembrances of women throughout eternity?"

"Yes," I replied. "Yes, of course I do. Copies from my scribes shall be dispersed. Other copies shall be buried in hidden areas – caves, mountains, and they will be protected against anyone doing harm to them." I thought about each hidden trove of her works surviving through the years. Even if most were destroyed – surely some would survive.

"Detractors in another time might wish to destroy them. Then I shall have been forgotten."

"We won't forget. Perhaps one day we shall be named after you or you isle."

She laughed briefly. As she pensively glanced away, there was a longing in her face. "Ah, if only a song or two survives, to tell my love, I would be satisfied. If only handfuls of my lyrics are passed along the centuries, a fragment at a time, I would feel satisfied."

"Your poetry is to be our fulfilled inheritance of love. Each generation discovers the past of ancients. It never ends, for research brings renewed portions of history. We shall search for your words, if need be."

She took my face between her hands and looked into my eyes. "I can't be certain that women in new generations will know me. But *you* now know me. And please, I implore you to share remembrance of me. As I shall remember you." She pressed a small cameo in her likeness into my hand. Into the other, she placed a golden coin on a chain. It was imprinted with her very image. "These must assist your memory when we are long parted - and far parted."

We walked to where the ship would be docked. I noticed she was becoming withdrawn. She was preparing to say goodbye. She had place thousands of words within my heart. As well as within my safekeeping, I would forever feel her presence and also her poetry of us.

"My bed tonight will be a somber chamber," she uttered.

"Without you, my heart will also fill with sorrow," I murmured. "I thank you for all you've done for me, and for the women of my land. The women of all lands," I corrected.

When the vessel came into sight, I cringed. I despised the oars and great sails of the ship that would take me from her side. Our caress was tighter than I knew possible. There were kisses of farewell. Then I left her arms.

Boarding, I fought the moment when I would turn and our glances would trade for the final time. Filled with longing, my forlorn sense of abandonment overwhelmed me. Her graceful carriage moved up onto the cliff where she could watch the ship for many miles. When she turned back to wave, my tears streamed.

As the ship set sail, I could hear the echoes of her voice. That voice whispered my name as it sang those lyrics. It also questioned if she might be forgotten.

My own reassurance - that the world would not disregard her - was now to become my mission. Perhaps another generation might attempt to obliterate her words. They might burn them, mutilate them, or throw them into the great oceans. Perhaps bury them in the great depths of earth.

But we shall not forget her. We shall continue searching her out.

For how could we forget last night?

She will always be the cherished poetess of those lovely lyrics. She is creator and builder of volumes of compositions about the spirit. Our spirit – with promises and pursuits – she sings *us*.

I was filled with the scent of wild rosemary. Visons of olive groves invaded my thought. Glowing words floated through me. Securely locked within my heart was the assurance and knowledge that I am a woman touched by her love.

I had fallen in love with Sappho. I knew not when. Was it many years ago when her lyrics came to me? Or was it when she held me throughout the night?

Why does the answer matter? We all fall in love with her poetry of us. Those lyrics take us within our celebration.

Kieran York

Author Kieran York

Kieran York

ABOUT THE AUTHOR

Kieran York has authored both Sapphic fiction and poetry. Her lesbian mystery series *Timber City Masks and Crystal Mountain Veils,* featuring Royce Madison were originally written and published in the mid-1990s. A second edition of them was recently released. *Shinney Forest Cloaks* is the third in the series.

In addition to *Within Our Celebration*, Kieran also wrote a collection of lesbian short fiction entitled *Sugar With Spice* that was published in 1989.

In 2012, York's book, *Appointment with a Smile,* was published and was a 2013 Lambda Literary Society Award Finalist in the category of Romance. Her next novel, *Careful Flowers,* was released in 2013, followed by two releases in 2014 – *Earthen Trinkets* and *Night Without Time,* published by Scarlet Clover Publishers. In 2015, *Touring Kelly's Poem, and Loitering on the Frontier* were released. Also planned in 2015 is a new mystery series titled *Trevar's Team: 1.*

In 2014, her volume of poetry, *Blushing Aspen,* was published as the Sappho's Corner Solo Poets book of poetry. It won The Rainbow Award Honorable Mention for poetry, and was a Finalist in the poetry category of Golden Crown Literary Awards. In 2015 the poetry book titled *Realm of Belonging* was published by Scarlet Clover Publishers.

York was also a contributor in *Sappho's Corner Poetry Series – Wet Violets, Volume 2; Roses Read, Volume 3; and Delectable Daisies, Volume 4.* This series is edited by Beth Mitchum.

Previously, during the seventies and eighties, Kieran worked as a reporter and reviewer for both newspapers and magazines, and was a newspaper publisher for three years. She also wrote and performed songs with a regional woman's band. She has been guest lecturer and panel member at various events, including Rocky Mountain Book Exhibition, Colorado Musicians Series, Sisters in Crime Mystery Writers, Mystery Writers of America, Inc. She is a member of Lambda Literary Society and Golden Crown Literary Society.

She has written for *Journal of Mystery Readers International.* In addition, she has given numerous campus and coffeehouse poetry readings, as well as taught poetry and creative writing workshops. She graduated from Fort Hays Kansas State University, and attended

Mexico's University of the Americas her junior year. She has done graduate work at the University of Colorado.

Kieran lives in the Rocky Mountain Foothills of Colorado with her schnauzer, Clover. She enjoys music, literature, and art. She considers her valuables to include Clover and her other family and friends, her library, her antique typewriter collection, and her guitar.

Additional information is available on her website:
http://kieranyork.com

Or the Scarlet Clover Publishers website:
http://www.scarletcloverpublishers.com

Or her Amazon Authors Page:
www.amazon.com/author/kieranyork/

Kieran York

COMING ATTRACTIONS:

TREVAR'S TEAM: 1

Beryl Trevar, Rachel Rosen, and Summer Wade are always on duty when it comes to an intriguing murder case. The Sapphic trio is an amazing blend of savvy, intelligence, sensuality, daring, and heart. They know how to use each element, and they also know how to use their Berettas.

They live in Palm Beach, Florida aboard a yacht. Each woman has an exciting, intricate, and entangled backstory. Each has her own reason for wanting to capture the badasses of the world.

The trio has another commonality. They all love women. They're all tough, bright, edgy, tender, gorgeous, and resilient. What more can main characters hope to be?

Their yacht is named *The Radclyffe-Hull*. Hmmmm. Well, then! Was the word *romantic* used in the trio's description? If not, it should have been.